HAUNTED
HERTFORD

HAUNTED
HERTFORD

Ruth Stratton

The
History
Press

With grateful thanks to Hertford Museum, a gem of the county town, whose little-known but extensive historical resources and photo archive have been invaluable to this work.

Aerial view of Hertford from All Saints' tower. (Hertford Museum collection)

First published 2012

The History Press
The Mill, Brimscombe Port
Stroud, Gloucestershire, GL5 2QG
www.thehistorypress.co.uk

ISBN 978 0 7524 8698 7
Typesetting and origination by The History Press
Printed in Great Britain

Contents

Foreword

ONE of the most common questions I am asked is whether I have ever seen a ghost. Unfortunately I haven't, but I have heard some, sensed and smelt many, and have often been within seconds of catching one! Perhaps this is what fuels my continuing fascination with the subject. In the course of my research for various books on ghosts, and during my work as a paranormal investigator, I have spoken to countless people who are unshakably convinced about their brushes with the supernatural in whatever form this has taken. I do believe ghosts exist and that there are many things we cannot yet explain. Perhaps in the future we will understand more about the ghost phenomenon but, for the present, it remains a tantalising mystery.

In the course of discussions with people who have experienced unexplained happenings, I am often asked for explanations. For this reason, I have enlisted the help of a fellow paranormal investigator to contribute his thoughts to some of the stories included in this book. These take the form of Ghost Hunter's Notes and an Endnote. These may put some readers' minds at rest, or at least provide food for thought for others. For those who simply delight in the thrill of a good ghost story, I hope you find plenty of shivers and chills in this book.

Acknowledgements

I would like to thank: Jean Riddell; Peter Ruffles, for invaluably capturing the changes in Hertford over the years; David Lee; Sara Taylor; Holly Rapley; Julie Sessions; Hertford Museum; David Poole; Dannii Cutmore; Ali and Nik Goodwin-Jones; Morris Cockman; Gavin Henderson; Ian Chivers; Andrew Newbury; Reg Edwards; Peter Brown; Nikki Wrangle; Nicholas Connell; Margaret Harris; Ian from Hertford; Les Middlewood; Steve Beeston; Denise Dilley; and also Greg, for enabling me to write on the move.

To all of those who have helped me but wish to keep their names out of print – thank you to you all, you know who you are!

Introduction

IT seems that people's thoughts naturally turn to ghosts as autumn approaches and the nights draw in. This is quite understandable, as this time has always been traditionally the 'season for ghosts'. However, the truth is that we are haunted all year round and ghosts don't just disappear when the clocks go forward.

Hertford is a town where layers of history sandwich each other – where behind one street there is another hidden street of treasures, and where inconspicuous doorways lead to unexpected amazing historical interiors. In this wonderful jumble of ancient properties, more have ghostly residents than not. So many shopkeepers,

Roofs from Gascoyne Way car park, July 1972. (Peter Ruffles' collection)

office staff, restaurateurs, homeowners and occupants have had spooky experiences that the population must be positively tripled by the number of ghostly souls still going about their business in the town. But before we peer into the haunted corners of ancient Hertford, with its castle and legends of secret tunnels, it is necessary to understand the history of this charming market town founded in Saxon times on the bank of the river Lea.

Hertford has a long and celebrated past. It is a town of alleys, yards, lanes, passages and slum areas. It is a royal borough, county and market town, as well as an industrial and commercial centre. One of Hertford's earliest written references was in the *Anglo-Saxon Chronicle* in AD 913, when King Edward the Elder created two fortifications known as burghs either side of its ford. The North Burgh was the area around Old Cross, whilst the South Burgh became the commercial centre around where

Shire Hall now stands, with market, shops and inns. Hertford developed as a Royal Mint and traded corn and flour to London. The town's importance as a royal burgh in medieval times, with its castle and royal residence, gave it its county town status. In 1441 King Henry VI granted Hertford its first charter, which established a market on Thursdays and Saturdays.

During the 1500s, royalty regularly visited the castle. The town at this time was described as a 'bustling dirty place, streets filled with animal manure and human waste and meat butchered out in the open'. With the Civil War in the 1600s came a period of tumult and unrest, and royalty no longer visited the town. By the 1800s, residential areas began to grow up and the railway brought an increase in trade and population. The Assizes, the County Parliamentary and the Borough elections were all held here.

Old Hertford had a lamplighter who emerged at dusk and before dawn with

The road that sliced Hertford in two. Gascoyne Way, view towards All Saints' Church. (Hertford Museum collection)

Pegs Lane before the Gascoyne Way.
(Hertford Museum collection)

his long hooked pole. In the early 1900s, a familiar figure in the town was F. W. Taylor, the Muffin Man, who carried a great wooden tray upon his cushioned head. There was also the knife grinder who set up shop on a doorstep, and the scrap metal merchant with his horse-drawn cart and cry of 'any old iron'.

In the 1960s, a relief road was constructed (amidst much controversy) which severed the old town in two. This road is the Gascoyne Way (named after the Gascoyne Cecil family of Hatfield House) and it had a catastrophic effect on many historical inns and buildings, which were swept away in the process. All Saints' churchyard was ripped in two and the back gardens of Fore Street and Castle Street were sliced up as the new route cut its way through people's homes and final resting places. According to local historian Eve Sangster, before the construction of the Gascoyne Way, Pegs Lane was a narrow country road 'with steep banks on both sides with primroses and cowslips and trees meeting overhead'. It is now a busy road separated from the older part of the town by unsightly 1960s buildings.

Despite its many changes, Hertford still carries a sense of its past into the twenty-first century, through its architecture and through the secrets of the souls which continue to haunt the streets and buildings of this charming market town.

Ruth Stratton, 2012

Pegs Lane after the Gascoyne Way, 1968. (Peter Ruffles' collection)

one

Bull Plain

IN a survey of 1620, Bull Plain was described as 'the way leading towards Little Hartham across the water', which is the edge of what is now Folly Island, accessed by the footbridge. At this time, the extensive Prince's Arms coaching inn stretched from No. 15 (currently Hertford Cameras) to the corner of Maidenhead Street, where it adjoined another inn called the Glove & Dolphin (currently Edinburgh Woollen Mill). After the Civil War in the mid-1600s, the Prince's Arms became the Bull, from which the area took its name. In 1857, with the decline of coach travel, the Bull inn was demolished leaving only the 'tap' to continue as the Bull (now In Depth and Hertford Cameras).

Bull Plain, 1904. (Hertford Museum collection)

The Bull. (Hertford Museum collection)

Six properties were recorded in this street in 1620. Entering from the modern Salisbury Square, Christopher White's house and garden were on the right; next was Elizabeth White's house, divided into two; then came a cottage 'newly erected' and backing onto Butcherie (or Butcherly) Green (today's Bircherley Green) and also divided. This property belonged to Mary Tooke and was what is now Tooke House and Hertford Museum (Nos 18 and 20 Bull Plain). On the west side was the house later called Waterside, owned by John Sharley or Shirley. This property was damaged in the Zeppelin raid of 1915 and was subsequently demolished. The clinic stands on part of its site. In 2012 this area was redeveloped, with a service road running alongside the clinic to a new library building.

Hertford Museum

Night at the museum

The recently refurbished museum is housed in an early seventeenth-century building at No. 18 Bull Plain and there have been many reports of ghosts here. The building, dating from around 1610, was originally one large house next door to No. 20, Tooke House. It is now divided in two. Tooke House takes its name from the builders of the block, Mary and William Tooke. Formerly shops

and business premises, No. 18 (known as Walton House) was purchased for £800 in 1913 from Thomas Pamphilon, and conversion work began in preparation for its opening as a museum in February 1914. The founders were two brothers and members of a very long-established family that came to Hertford in the seventeenth century. These were Robert Thornton Andrews and William Frampton Andrews. Echoes of their influence in the town can be found in some of the street names on nearby Folly Island. They had previously opened a museum at 54–56 Fore Street in 1903, before the collection was moved to Bull Plain in 1914. Internally, little remains from the 1610 period except for the upper flight of stairs leading to the attic, and it is here that many people have reported experiencing ghostly activity.

In April 2006, a visitor to the museum told staff about the female ghost he saw standing at the top of the first-floor staircase. He described her as Edwardian, wearing a high collar and with bright red hair piled upon her head. This description was repeated by a husband and wife who came to visit the museum from Norfolk two years later in 2008. Other visitors have seen this ghost, sometimes bareheaded and sometimes wearing a bonnet. Some people

Rear view of Hertford Museum and allotments (now Bircherley Green service yard). (Hertford Museum collection)

have also reported seeing children hanging about on the stairs to the attic. The most recent sighting is of a little boy, about nine years old, in Victorian clothing. He was seen by a visitor in May 2007, running up the stairs and laughing mischievously.

In March 2012, the lift between floors began mysteriously operating by itself, despite it needing keys to be unlocked so it can start. The front-of-house staff had the key and the lift was locked, but somehow it had sent itself to the floor above. No one could explain how this had been possible.

During my time working at the museum as Assistant Curator between 2005 and 2010, I ran a number of ghost walks around the town at Halloween as a fundraising activity for the museum. Arriving early on the night of the very first tour, I sat quietly on my own in the building, having a cup of tea and revising my notes. The building was empty and idly I glanced at the CCTV monitor which showed the upstairs display areas in semi-darkness. I noticed a couple of times that a bright white light seemed to appear and fly around the room. After the walk, the group came back to the museum for tea, biscuits and to exchange ghostly tales. A group of ladies belonging to a spiritualist group disappeared upstairs. Later, when closing up, I found the ladies sitting in the dark in the children's activity room, saying that they were aware of an active female presence in this area of the building.

In 2009 the museum went through a major redevelopment: often the catalyst for an increase in ghostly activity. This seemed like the perfect opportunity to

No. 18 Bull Plain prior to 1913, when the Andrews brothers purchased the building for the museum. The name of Pamphilon can be seen above the window. The frontage is little changed today. (Hertford Museum collection)

Museum staircase to the attic, dating from 1610. (Hertford Museum collection)

carry out an overnight paranormal investigation. The museum closed its doors for refurbishment on Christmas Eve 2008, and the investigation was planned for the following January. So, on 31 January 2009, the NightWatch UK paranormal investigation team assembled at the museum. With the rooms emptied of their display cases and the attic's vast collections of photographs and paper archives removed to safe storage, the rooms of the building were strangely bare and hollow. The group was joined by celebrated clairvoyant Marion Goodfellow, who walked around each room in turn, picking up echoes of the many layers of the building's history. As stated in the rules of the group, no one is told where the investigation will be held; this is to ensure that no prior research can be carried out to falsify the findings. Team members were told to meet at a nearby service station and were then given directions from there on the night, so they only knew the destination

once they had actually arrived in Hertford. Marion Goodfellow was no exception.

In the kitchen area, Marion immediately sensed two raggedy little Victorian boys aged between six and eight, who sat huddled in a corner, their arms around their knees. This area had housed a Victorian extension before it was demolished in the 1980s to make a kitchen and staff offices.

Beside the front door, Marion sensed that someone called Nancy once lived here. Nancy wore black lace-up boots, a long panel skirt and an early Victorian bustle which was gathered at the side. She wore a blouse with long 'leg of mutton' sleeves and a cross-over pinafore. Accompanying Nancy was the smell of bread, as if a bakery was nearby. Marion felt that Nancy had something to do with the Women's Union and that the downstairs had strong connections with religious meetings and official gatherings. Research shows that No. 20 was sold to Miss Thornton in 1884 and the Mission Room was built. Around 1932 the Mission Room became All Saints' Mission Hall and also accommodated a branch of the Oddfellows. This is an order of friendly societies set up in the eighteenth century to protect and assist its members at a time when there was no welfare state, trade unions or National Health Service. Marion also felt that a man named Thomas lived here. This is a very general statement and a common name, but could she be referring to Thomas Pamphilon whose family occupied the house before it was sold to be the museum in 1913? It becomes a little more convincing in a moment.

At the top of the stairs, Marion picked up a male energy who was angry about the changes. She felt he was from the early Victorian period and had been involved in some way with the coal-mining industry and was quite well-to-do. Could this be related to one of the founders of the museum, either R. T. or W. F. Andrews? Research reveals that in the 1800s Samuel Andrews, their grandfather, operated barges on the Lee Navigation from Hertford and began trading in coal, which was much sought after in an area that was far away from a coalfield. Samuel also had a farm at nearby Rush Green and another at Bramfield. In addition, he ran a timber business and owned brickfields. Samuel was indeed quite an entrepreneur.

On the upper floors, Marion was now being told off by Thomas for being in the family's drawing room. Thomas Pamphilon had a plumbing business and shop which occupied the downstairs rooms of the premises, the upstairs being the family's private living quarters, including their drawing room. The feeling of children was prevalent in the upper rooms. Marion felt that one room in particular was attracting them. This, she believed, was a room filled with toys. Indeed, this had formerly been the museum's activity room, where children had toys to play with, school groups came to do workshops and holiday activities were organised. According to Marion, the toys had been attracting children from the past to that room. She could hear them singing nursery rhymes. Another member of the team, Andy Matthews, joined her with his voice recorder to see if he could pick up any voices from the past. They sat in the shadowy silence of the empty room and he switched on his recording device. At 9.49 p.m. there came three knocks followed by one more knock. Andy played back the recording and it had picked up the knocks. But it had also picked up something else; something that had not been audible to him or Marion as they sat waiting in the darkness. Very faintly they heard a child's voice, as if it was coming from a long way away, up through a tunnel: 'Here we are.'

Andy encouraged the voices to communicate. He switched on the recorder once more and began singing the first lines to a nursery rhyme. He paused to allow them to fill in the missing words before pressing playback on the machine. Sure enough, the little voices came straining through the time tunnel and recorded the exact missing lines of the nursery rhyme. There was no other noise in the room at the time; there were no voices from outside that could have been misinterpreted as children from a long way off. It was very eerie. Interestingly, documentation states that sometime between 1893 and 1913, a school was housed here.

In the attic Marion was joined by a man with a bowl haircut of black hair, smoking a pipe, who went by the name of Frederick Fosdyke. He told her, 'From here I can see the clock and I saw the crane fall over.' At one time, according to Frederick, you could see the sky through the top of the attic, as it was in a dilapidated state.

In the cellar, Marion felt there was a Roman connection to the site long before No. 18 was built. She believes it was a traffic thoroughfare, and a street market would have been close by with livestock kept on the site where the cellar stands now. There was indeed a cattle market in the near vicinity, behind the Ram Inn along Fore Street.

Walking around the building, Marion and Andy both felt that the interior would have had a lot more rooms, but there was also a feeling of open space. This was true of a time before the internal walls were removed for constructing the museum: the house adjoined with No. 20, and would have had around fifteen rooms. Then, when the house was converted to a museum, walls and chimney stacks were removed to create three spacious display rooms.

Andy sensed bomb damage had occurred here and questioned whether the building had been involved in any such thing. Just yards away, on 13 October 1915, a Zeppelin L16 had dropped fourteen high-explosive and thirty incendiary bombs on Hertford. The third high-explosive bomb fell nearby, outside the entrance of Lombard House, the Conservative Club, killing six people.

It's worth mentioning here that many museums have the reputation of being haunted and it has been suggested that these spirits may be connected not to the buildings but to the collections themselves. In 1988 the decision was made to transform the small garden behind the museum into a Jacobean Knot Garden. In the course of this work, a pillar box and a stone coffin were unearthed and moved to the museum to be added to the collection. With the museum housing so many ancient objects with long and varied histories, who could be surprised at finding the odd ghost clinging to something that may have been very important to them?

Ghost Hunter's Notes: This is a great example of an EVP recording. The method of using the nursery rhymes is also very sound practice. A lot of investigators forget to tailor their techniques based on the results they are getting on the evening. Here

First-floor museum galleries in 1918, showing how the internal walls were removed to open up the rooms. R.T. Andrews is seated. (Hertford Museum collection)

the medium is picking up on children, so speaking to the entities like they are children makes sense. I have often seen on TV ghost hunters going to foreign countries and 'calling out' to ghosts in their own languages. This would not get as good results as using the languages that the ghosts would have used when they were alive.

Beadle House

Doctor in the house

Beadle House, at No. 16 Bull Plain, stands next door to the museum. One witness to ghostly activity here was alone in the basement one day when she heard someone breathing close by and sensed she was not alone. She ran upstairs and related to her colleagues what had just happened. She was told that the previous cleaners had left because they had seen a man walking down the stairs wearing what was described as an old doctor's outfit with a long cape and doctor's bag. They had also heard unexplained noises and the replacement cleaner had watched chairs moving by themselves. On a separate occasion, another employee at Beadle House was working in the basement when she saw a lady dressed in a long, mustard-coloured dress of the Georgian period.

Beadle House was originally called Dimsdale House because, in 1703/4, it was sold unfinished by Sarah Crowch to Alderman John Dimsdale, the relative of Baron Dimsdale, an early advocate of vaccination. John was also a doctor, so perhaps this is the character seen walking down the stairs? The site previously accommodated three cottages bought by Sarah in 1701 from Walter Dickenson, perhaps converted from part of Elizabeth White's houses or built in her garden. In 1831, the Literary & Scientific Institution took over the house. A century later, it was in bad repair and was used as a factory. In 1946 it was acquired for redevel-

Bull Plain with Folly Bridge ahead, after the Zeppelin raid of 13 October 1915. (Hertford Museum collection)

opment but was saved by receiving a Grade II listing, and a preservation order was placed on the building. Evidence found by members of East Herts Archaeological Society suggests that Beadle House was an older property which had been largely rebuilt. In the early 1970s it was purchased by Beadle Property Holdings, which gave the building its current name; it was restored in 1974, receiving the European Architectural Year Award in 1975. Today the building houses a collection of shared office space by different businesses.

Lombard House

Ghostly games at Old Henry's home
This building houses the Hertford Club. Established in 1878, the Hertford Club is the only private members club in Hertford. The building is Grade II listed and is thought to have been a fifteenth-century hall, providing lodgings for the Assize judges. It was extended in the seventeenth century and renovated in the 1980s after a fire.

Lombard House was once the home of Hertfordshire historian Sir Henry Chauncy, who wrote the *Historical Antiquities of Hertfordshire* in 1700, thus staff at the Hertford Club refer to their ghost as 'Old Henry', though it is not certain that this is the restless spirit of the man himself. Henry Chauncy

was also the recorder at the trial of Jane Wenham in Hertford in 1712. Jane was the last reputed witch in England sentenced to hang, but she was pardoned, and her trial did much to bring about the repeal of the Witchcraft Act in 1736.

Creaking floorboards and footsteps have been heard when there is no one there. Moreover, the barman returned to work to open up at 6 p.m. one evening and heard laughter and male voices coming from the snooker room. He thought perhaps he had locked someone in earlier when he'd shut up for the afternoon. When he went into the snooker room, the cues were in their racks, quivering, and the balls were scattered on the table, as if a phantom game of snooker had just been abandoned.

Shenval Press

'The man you just described is a dead man'
Shenval Press stood in Parliament Square, occupying the building which is now the Job Centre. It has been described as very old and eerie by people who have worked there. Many people have experienced ghostly activity over the years. The following story was related by a Hertford councillor and occurred in the late 1950s or early '60s.

Charles Bazin (Charlie) was a bachelor who lived in London with his sister. However, during the week, when working at Shenval Press, he lodged in a boarding house in North Road, Hertford, returning home to London at weekends. He died suddenly in the waiting room at Hertford North station in the mid-1950s, whilst waiting for the train to take him back to London.

Mick Wilson came to work at Shenval Press after leaving his home in South Africa and moving to Harlow in the 1950s.

No. 18 Bull Plain showing Dimsdale House (derelict) and Hertford Museum next door, c. 1972. (Hertford Museum collection)

Dimsdale House, 1965. (Peter Ruffles' collection)

18

On Wednesday nights he worked as duty reader on *Time & Tide*, an independent weekly newspaper printed at Simson Shand (trading as the Shenval Press). He had never seen, met or even heard of Charlie Bazin.

On the night concerned, Mick had just read some copy proof and taken it downstairs to the compositor for corrections. He returned to the reading room via the single rickety wooden staircase, which was the only way of accessing the reading department. On entering, he noticed a man whom he did not recognise sitting at one of the desks at the far end of the room. Mick assumed that he was one of the men from the machine room, who had come to look out of the window to see what was happening in Parliament Square; this was quite common practice so he thought no more about it. The man looked up but did not speak. Mick nodded his acknowledgement of the fellow and went to his own desk to continue working. After a while Mick realised he had heard no sound from the man at the other end of the room and got up to see if all was OK. But the man was not there. This was very strange as Mick's desk was beside the staircase – the only means of entry and exit – so it would have been impossible for the man to have left without Mick noticing.

Lombard House at the end of Bull Plain, 1935. (Hertford Museum collection)

He went downstairs to the compositor, John Edwards, and asked if he had seen anyone come down the stairs. John replied, 'The only person I have seen pass up and down the stairs is you.' John then asked Mick to describe the man, which he did. One thing he had particularly noticed was that the man had been wearing a hat. After hearing Mick's description, John felt fairly certain that the man he had just described was a dead man. It fitted Charlie Bazin perfectly, and Charlie had always worn a hat to work.

Mick was a strong, confident person who thought nothing of walking from Harlow to Hertford to work on a daily basis. But, from that night onwards, he refused to work night shifts alone in the reading department.

Young ladies who worked in the office did not like working alone in the filing room, which was adjacent to the reading room. They complained of a 'strange feeling'. One female worker had her first job there aged fifteen in the early 1960s. She describes it as:

A huge place with over 200 people working there. There were rooms full of compositors, tappers, setters; it ran all the way along the back of the Co-op and came out in a little yard behind a fruit shop. There were backways, stairways, nooks and crannies. I came through the machine minders one Friday morning and there was a tiny, narrow twisting staircase at the back and climbing up there it was ever so eerie; dark, narrow and twisty and covered in cobwebs. It hadn't been swept in years! That's where the ghost had been seen.

The building had formerly been a bell foundry, and part of the building at the rear was once stables complete with a sloping

Parliament Square, showing the Simson Shand building behind the war memorial. (Hertford Museum collection)

Parliament Row, looking south; a closer view of the Simson Shand building. (Hertford Museum collection)

cobbled floor. A former member of staff remembers the tunnels which ran beneath Simson Shand. She says, 'I went down there one day but it was a bit scary. The paper used to come in and they used to do the packing down in the basement. It was all cellars and tunnels, like something out of Guy Fawkes!' Simson Shand moved to Harlow in the late 1970s.

Ghost Hunter's Notes: Tunnels are a common talking point in Hertford, and in recent years there have been many rumours about the tunnels being linked with the Knights Templar, a mysterious order of warrior monks who went to the Holy Land in support of the crusaders, only to return to Europe wealthy and believed to be in possession of some of the most famous holy relics, most notably the Holy Grail. Conspiracy theorists have recently highlighted Hertford, especially the tunnels, as a possible hiding place for the Grail. This could be due to the proximity of Hertford to Temple Dinsley, Preston, a stronghold of the Templars in the UK. When the Templars fell out of favour with the King, the Dinsley Templars were imprisoned in Hertford Castle, yet their treasures were never discovered. Local legend in Preston states that 'an ancient oak to the east side of a pool, long ago filled in, is a clue to the resting place of fabulous treasure'. Maybe it is still out there to be found.

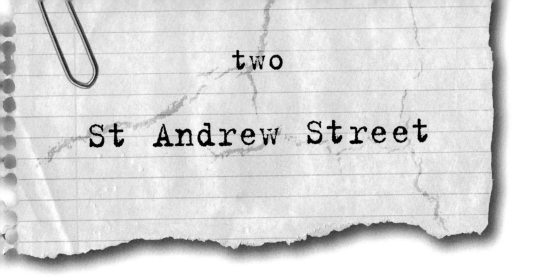

two

St Andrew Street

S T Andrew Street is a charming mix of historical buildings, alleyways and yards, retaining the age and character of the past. At night it is lit by modern bulbs in the original gas lamps, giving the street the feeling of being largely unchanged in over 100 years. Many of the buildings are from the eighteenth and nineteenth centuries, and the roofline dips and falls in a delightful jumble. Look out for Yeomanry House, built in the 1700s, which is architecturally of interest. The most spectacular

St Andrew Street. The Verger's House, now Beckwith Antiques Centre. (Hertford Museum collection)

'Quality Street', looking east with the horse trough on the left; the Verger's House is on the right. (Hertford Museum collection)

building in the street, though, is Beckwith Antiques Centre which overhangs the pavement. This was formerly the Verger's House, built around 1450, and is the oldest surviving domestic building in Hertford.

St Andrew Street is now mainly commercial and there is a wonderful feeling of neighbourly community between the shop owners. There is an air of people feeling privileged to have a business in this historic street, often known as 'Quality Street'. The first detailed information available for St Andrew Street is from a trade directory of 1822, when it was the centre for specialised crafts. It was the only street in the county where there was a distillery. It was also the centre for umbrella manufacture, which was unique in the county. It then became predominantly a street for antique dealers.

Wallace House

Night stake-out at naturalist's home
Wallace House is so called because it was once the home of celebrated naturalist Alfred Russel Wallace. Wallace is documented to have developed the theory of evolution around the same time as Darwin. Unknown to each other, both men had been working along parallel lines of thought and reached the revolutionary theory in different ways. Darwin received a letter from Wallace describing theories he himself had already conceived, but it was Darwin who published and received the credit for the theory that rocked the Victorian world.

In around 1828 the Wallace family lived in one part of the house whilst a family called Silk lived in the larger part. Wallace said of the town in which he grew up:

'The old town of Hertford, where I first obtained a rudimentary acquaintance with my fellow creatures, is perhaps one of the most pleasantly situated county towns in England.'

Wallace House is a warren of a building, currently housing a doctor's practice. The building was converted from two houses, Nos 9 and 11 St Andrew Street, in the early 1980s. On the other side of Wallace House is the entrance to the public car park and there was once another ancient house here, the Red House, the charity house of Alderman Carde, which was destroyed by fire in 1936.

During renovation work on the building, builders found that drills started up on their own and a shovel moved across the room of its own accord. Many strange events took place during the construction work and builders did not like being there at all. Cleaners have worked a night and then refused to come back again because the building is 'haunted' and, during the building work, staff witnessed objects flying across the room.

Figures have been seen wandering along the top-floor corridor when there has been no one there. A new reception manager was working in a glass-fronted office on the top floor one afternoon when she glanced across into the common room opposite. A man was standing in the corner looking out of the window. She described him as distinguished-looking with white hair and a black frock-coat. As she watched, the figure gradually evaporated from the bottom upwards.

One evening, around 6 p.m., Denise Dilley, the practice manager at the time, was working in her office when a large television set launched itself from the top of a filing cabinet and flew diagonally across the room, landing in front of the door. Denise said the TV had not been moved for about ten years, and the amazing thing was that the pot plant on top of it didn't even topple or spill out! Denise called for help from the evening cleaner and he became her witness to events. Together they carried the TV set into the cellar.

In the loft space above Denise's office, there was often the sound of something being dragged across the floor, but, on investigation, nothing could be found to explain the noise. However, it seems that the top corridor is the main problematic area. No one has liked working there alone at night and cleaners have refused to work up there alone. An elderly gentleman has been seen walking slowly along the corridor past the common room late at night; the sound of someone jumping up and down on the top floor has echoed down to the doctor's office below; and a knocking has been heard inside the practice manager's office when no one is in that room.

One member of staff did not like going down to the filing cabinets stored in the building's basement. She heard footsteps follow her down the steps and saw someone walk past her. When she had finished and went back upstairs, everyone seemed to be present and she asked who it was that had gone downstairs. No one knew of anyone going to the filing cabinets, so she went back down to see who her mysterious companion had been. There was no one there.

In September 2009, a paranormal investigation team staged a night's stake-out in Wallace House. As usual, only one member of the team knew the location and kept it from the others until they arrived in Hertford that evening. Pens kept disappearing and the team could all sense the tall, severe, frock-coated man with a long slab-like face and high forehead. A ten-year-old girl was also sensed, who was afraid of 'the lady' because she punished her. 'The lady', it seemed, was not happy about the ghost team invading her space. During a séance in the early hours, the clairvoyant Marion Goodfellow picked up the spirit of a man calling himself Alfred Watson. Could this be the misheard name of Alfred Wallace?

In 2012 a lady living on the opposite side of the street was awake in the early hours one morning. She stood at her window with a cup of tea, looking out at the empty St Andrew Street below her. Suddenly she noticed the figure of a man standing in the window of Wallace House above the archway, looking out. Surprised to see anyone there at that time of the morning, she popped into the surgery the next day to mention it to the receptionist. Whilst the surgery admitted that occasionally one doctor will work a late shift, it was found that no one was on duty that night and certainly wouldn't still be working at the hour the man was seen.

One of the buildings which has been amalgamated into the maze that is Wallace House was formerly the Cranbourne Arms Inn, which stood at No. 5 (now adjoining the Paddyfields restaurant at No. 3). This became a pub around 1850 and traded for over 100 years until its licence was extinguished in 1954. If you look carefully at the buttress to the right of the front-door arch, you can just make out the words of the pub name in the brickwork. The pub was a working man's local. The following is a description given by a lad on his first visit to the pub with his father:

> It was a little tiny pub, very dark and smoky. I went in with him [dad] and he immediately shook hands with the landlord. I thought – this is odd, he never shakes hands with anybody. I wasn't a drinker, I was very young and it turned out that he was a Buff; a member of the old Buffaloes. They were a secret society, poor man's

Masons. They have a special way of shaking hands and every time I went with him I used to look very closely to see what they did. He never told me of course.

Perhaps some of the activity in Wallace House can be attributed to those drinkers of the tiny Cranbourne Arms.

No. 19

Still clocking on

Number 19 (originally in a block with Nos 17, 21 and 23) is a late fifteenth-century building extended in the seventeenth century with alterations made in the nineteenth. The shop is currently a beauty salon. Susan Brown, who worked at No. 19, related that the strange noises from the first floor were from a nineteenth-century clockmaker who was still working. (Ralph Lawler, the clockmaker, occupied the building from the 1840s to the 1890s.) Susan also reports that the ghost of a little white dog has been seen in Tamworth Road. The dog was owned by Mrs Brett from No. 26, who was killed in the land mine that fell in the garden of No. 24.

No. 4 – Vogue Hairdressers

James' story

Vogue is housed in a building dating from 1578. It is haunted by a small man called James, aged around forty, dressed in black breeches, white socks, a tricorn hat and a black waistcoat with brass buttons. He likes shiny objects and the hair salon has suffered missing scissors and teaspoons. However, when staff ask for things to be returned, James helpfully obliges. If upset, James has been known to move furniture and throw Christmas cards

St Andrew Street, showing Vogue hairdresser and Hertfordshire Graphics next door. (Hertford Museum collection)

around the room. He is often seen by staff walking through the building, but everyone seems comfortable with his presence. It is said that James was once a porter with no living family. He lost his job and found himself with no money to pay his rent and no one to turn to, so took to hiding in the building's cellar.

Ghost Hunter's Notes: This story illustrates the potential to talk directly to ghosts. A lot of the time people presume talking to ghosts is impossible; however, there have been lots of cases where people have been able to speak directly to a ghost to get it to stop behaving in a certain way or to do a certain thing. Although speaking to ghosts normally only works with active/spirit-type entities, should anyone feel threatened or pestered by paranormal activity, it is always worth talking out loud and politely asking the ghost to stop; it works more often than not.

No. 6

George's games at the Graphics

Next door to Vogue is a shop which, until very recently, was Hertfordshire Graphics Ltd. Staff reported that tools would go missing and they heard someone talking to them who said his name was George. A member of staff, who sometimes worked late, heard footsteps climbing the stairs and stop outside his office. Other staff would not hang about when locking up, but would shut the door quickly and leave. Keys would move around and things would disappear. One day, a newly purchased book of stamps vanished just as a member of staff was about to use them. He asked aloud, 'George, put the stamps back!' and the stamps were back. After the business was sold, the next owner had the same problems, particularly

Mill Bridge after the V-1 flying bomb, 2 July 1944. (Hertford Museum collection)

with the stamps and with creaking stairs. Apparently the new owners were compelled to call the ghost 'George' also, and, when they asked for the stamps back, they received two sets. Obviously George had a sense of humour. Only one person claimed to have seen George and this was a clerk who had only been with the company three weeks and hadn't heard anything about the ghost. One day he asked who the old gentleman was in the long raincoat who stands at the end of the passage. He'd tried to talk to him, but the old man had just vanished.

It is believed that before the area was damaged by a doodlebug on Mill Bridge, Nos 2, 4 and 6 had all formed one property. During building work, Wigginton's (now the Women's Society Boutique at No. 2) was found to have fragile lath and plaster walls stuffed with red cow hair.

No. 20a

Ghostly goings-on at the Garrett

The flat above No. 20 can be accessed at street level by a brown front door numbered 20a. Chopped and changed a great deal over the years, this accommodation housed a family and nine children in 1901. Number 20 was described in a survey as a nineteenth-century timber-framed and stuccoed building with twentieth-century shop front and alterations. Number 20a was called the Garrett.

A previous occupant, who moved out in 2011, complained of feeling a pressure on her chest whilst lying in bed. When Ali and Nik Goodwin-Jones moved in just before Christmas 2011, Ali immediately sensed that the property was haunted. Soon after taking up residence, the couple returned home one day to find that the kitchen tap was running full on. This happened more than once. On another occasion, their daughter returned to the empty flat to find the bathroom tap running. She phoned Ali on her mobile and asked why this was happening. Ali said that no one had left the tap on. These occurrences only ceased when Ali asked aloud for the activity to stop, saying, 'We're on a water meter you know!'

Whilst watching TV in the lounge in the evenings, Ali and Nik have both heard a loud tapping at the window. This is an old sash window which looks out onto a yard and can only be accessed by a sloping roof. Ali says the tapping is loud enough to be heard above the TV and is an insistent noise, like someone trying to be let in. Thuds and the noise of someone moving around can be heard in the hallway in the middle of the night. When either of the couple has got up to check, there has been no one around and no reason for the noises.

Ali describes the general feeling in the flat as that of not being alone, and of instinctively sensing that someone is about to come into the room. The couple's cat sometimes behaves very strangely, staring intently at something they cannot see. There is a set of old cupboards in the lounge, believed to belong to previous occupants when the building was Pearl Assurance chartered accountants. These cupboards seem to bother the cat intensely. He goes mad at them trying to get inside and then sits staring at them without moving.

Ali has experienced shadows, lights flitting out of the corner of her eye, strange noises and things disappearing. She also feels there is something behind the walled-up doorway in the lounge. As she spoke to me, she saw the image of an old man in a waistcoat sitting in a chair with his sleeves rolled up. Could this be one of her ghostly flatmates? Ali believes there is more than one.

St Andrew Street, 1964. On the left is Pearl Assurance, in what is now 20a, the Garrett. (Peter Ruffles' collection)

No. 25 – Rigsby's Guest House

Uninvited guests

Number 25 St Andrew Street was built around 1750 and is a Grade II listed building. In 2012 it is a guesthouse with elegant accommodation more than nodding to the historical features of the building. Bathrooms have the original fireplaces from when the rooms were bedrooms, and right up in the eaves is a loft room complete with 200-year-old timbers. Secret staircases and creaking floors make this a fascinating building to explore. Perhaps the star feature, however, is the curved open staircase in the hall. Dating from the early 1800s, it is magnificently elegant and would not look amiss in an episode of *Upstairs Downstairs*.

The manager, Morris Cockman, lives on the premises with his wife. One morning his wife came downstairs looking bemused.

Attic room at Rigsby's Guest House, showing original timbers. (Courtesy of Morris Cockman)

She said she had heard someone walking around in the next room and assumed it was Morris. But she had found the room empty and Morris was actually downstairs at the time. Noises are also often heard from the linen store above the dining room. This was once a parlour room. Morris tells of the sound of footsteps and says it's common for things to move about in the building when no one else is present.

In recent times this building has had both commercial and residential usage. For many years it was an antique shop, one of the many in St Andrew Street. The rear buildings were once primitive barns. One of them had seen use as a tea shop, but during wartime was used to show films and newsreels. The main house was owned by many a prestigious landowner in its early years but was used for a long period by the Young Women's Christian Alliance.

Sweeping staircase at Rigsby's Guest House. (Courtesy of Morris Cockman)

Yeomanry House

Old Vic

Yeomanry House, built around 1725, has twentieth-century alterations and extensions. Now the centre for the Territorial Army, this Grade II listed building is haunted by something which has made hardened soldiers too afraid to be alone here at night.

Company Sergeant Major Reg Edwards, who lives in the caretaker's house on adjacent Dimsdale Street, would often work in the building at night. When it came to leaving, he would turn off the lights, lock the doors and walk back across the yard towards his home. But, on turning around on one occasion, he noticed a light remaining on in the top of the house. Feeling certain he had extinguished all the lights, Reg returned to Yeomanry House and turned the light off, checking the room was in darkness as he locked up. Then, once again walking across the yard, he looked over his shoulder and was horrified to see the light back on again. Reg said the building was most definitely empty so it wasn't someone playing tricks on him.

Permanent staff instructor Peter Brown refused to go into the building at night following a strange experience. He was in one

No. 28 St Andrew Street, 1956. The building once known as Wisteria House is now Yeomanry House, headquarters of the TA. (Hertford Museum collection)

of the offices when he heard footsteps on the stairs and the jangling of keys. He called out but there was no response. A short while later, he telephoned the caretaker Betty Edwards in the house across the yard, and asked her why she had come into the building and not announced her presence to him. Betty replied that she had not left her house all evening. Peter was a tough, experienced soldier but he was completely spooked by the event. Peter isn't the only one to have heard the footsteps and jangling keys. Commonly the phenomenon occurs between 6 and 7 p.m. Additionally, the sudden and unaccountable smell of strong tobacco has been experienced by some of the staff and visitors to the building, but not everyone smells it at the same time.

Former caretaker Vic dropped dead at the bottom of the dog-leg staircase in Yeomanry House foyer in around 1974. He was a heavy smoker. Could it be his ghost that so many have experienced, smoking his cigarette and jangling his keys as he does a ghostly round of the building? Reg's final comment on the building is that he is 'convinced' it is haunted.

The caretaker's house, built in the 1950s on an orchard, was previously used as the Home Guard Office canteen. It is also haunted. Doors open by themselves, and objects disappear and sometimes never reappear again. At the time of writing, Reg Edwards is waiting patiently for his book on Bulgaria to return, after it vanished from the footstool where he left it a few days previously. Reg says disappearing objects are only too common. There are odd creaking sounds and footsteps overhead, and the resident dog suddenly barks and growls at something unseen. Reg's grandson refuses to sleep upstairs, saying it is haunted, and will only sleep on the sofa in the lounge.

Three Tuns

Beware of the ghost!

Prior to the seventeenth century, the Three Tuns (now a Thai restaurant on the corner of Brewhouse Lane) was an alehouse called the Black Lion. The inn, first mentioned in 1781, was in two parts, the front dating from 1700 whilst the rear was older. A lintel over the fireplace in the bar is believed to be an original timber from Hertford Castle.

Most activity seems to have occurred in the back part of the building, beside the ladies' toilet. Staff reported objects moving about all the time, glasses jumping off the bar and things going missing with more than coincidental frequency. But most often seen was the bedraggled spectre of a young girl, who passed through a wall in the bar then climbed a non-existent staircase to the upstairs. When it was a pub, the staff didn't seem to be bothered by the haunting; in fact, a sign on the toilet read: 'Beware of the ghost!'

A newspaper article of April 2006 reported that a collector of old postcards had discovered something very unusual about a picture he had of St Andrew Street. The postcard from 1905 depicted a traditional image of people dressed in Edwardian clothing, going about their business in the street, or clustered in groups looking curiously at the camera. But in the middle of the street is what looks like a small smudge or human figure. Collector David Porthouse says: 'It looks like a twelve to fourteen-year-old girl who is barefoot. She has her hair parted and it looks as if she is carrying something.' Could this be the same poor girl from the Three Tuns, captured on camera at the turn of the century?

There has always been some confusion with the Three Tuns' ghost being that of a young girl who died in the St Andrew Street workhouse, which was thought to have originally been on the site of the Three Tuns. However, the workhouse had

St Andrew Street, the Three Tuns public house. (Hertford Museum collection)

St Andrew Street postcard, showing the smudgy ghost-like figure. (Hertford Museum collection)

never been on that site but was in fact built in 1724 on the Hertingfordbury Road. The building had been paid for by Collett of Hertford Castle, whose eventual heir was John Moses Carter, who also owned the Three Tuns. The deeds mention both properties, hence the confusion.

Bell & Shears

To keep the witches out

The house next door to the Three Tuns is another timber-framed building. There is a room here in which residents have felt they are being watched. When the building was being converted in around 2009, an historical artefact was discovered under the floor: a mummified cat placed to look towards the door, complete with collar, a hand-carved wooden flute, flowers and a crucifix around its neck. A mysterious local woman warned the builders to put it back as it keeps vampires and evil spirits away. Since the removal of the cat, the builders and occupants have reported strange noises and mysterious banging sounds inside the building.

This house once adjoined No. 38, where circular witch-marks have been etched onto the wood panelling by the door. These emblems were believed to prevent the entry of witches and evil spirits into the building. Sometimes they could also be found carved beside fireplaces. Number 38 has a room at the top of the shop which members of the public have disliked going into; they have complained of a very strange feeling there.

Historical records state that Nos 36 and 38 were originally together in a block and date from the early eighteenth century, with alterations in the nineteenth and twentieth centuries. Number 38 was built on the foundations of an inn called Bell Mould in around 1625, which became known as Little Bell, later Bell & Shears. The 1600s were a time when the witch craze was at its height.

Ghost Hunter's Notes: There are many items that were, in the past, concealed in houses: shoes, witches' bottles, symbols, and even dried or mummified animals. The belief is that these were positioned near places of weakness or entry to the house, such as a doorway or window, or in a central location such as a fireplace, as a ward against evil spirits entering the house. Cats held special significance because, in life, they were respected for their hunting prowess and were supposed to possess psychic powers. These skills make cats especially good as protectors from other-worldly intruders.

Fred Roche's Shoe Shop

Unhappy spirit who couldn't leave
At the west end of St Andrew Street, where all the shops peter out into the relief road, once stood Fred Roche's shoe shop. The business closed in the mid-2000s and reverted back to being a domestic cottage. During its time as his shoe shop, owner Eddie (Fred) Roche felt that the building was an unhappy place. Eddie said, 'This is definitely a haunted house. I am a Christian but I don't like coming in here at night.'

Eddie's brother Andrew recalls:

> I lived here on my own for five years and at midnight on a regular basis I used to hear someone running up the stairs. The footsteps stopped outside my door and then I'd hear them running back down again, but when I looked, there would be nobody there. There was no one next door who it could have been. At the time, there was a doctor's surgery next door.

Andrew remembers another night in particular:

> I awoke very, very cold and there was a figure perched on the end of my bed where my chest of drawers was. It was a woman. She sat there looking and me and then disappeared! It was horrifying. She was very small and was wearing a head-scarf or veil.

The image jogged a memory of something he and his sister had seen when they were young. It was the figure of a small old lady walking down the stairs and through the wall. 'She was following the old route of the stairs,' Andrew recalls. The family had indeed altered the route of the stairs when they turned the house into a shop. The ghost became a regular sight after that. Linen was stacked and removed by invisible hands, as if a bed was being made up. According to one of the shop's customers, Andrew's description of the figure matched that of a former resident, and the old lady is believed to have lived in the cottage before going off to South Africa, where she was swindled out of her savings. When she came back to Britain, she was very unhappy and she transferred that feeling indelibly to the building.

In the 1960s, many ancient properties were demolished at the west end of the street to make way for the Gascoyne Way relief road. Fred Roche's shop and the neighbouring cottage escaped this mass destruction and remain among the few surviving examples of this humblest sort of town cottage, with one storey and an attic.

Fred Roche's shoe shop, 1974. (Peter Ruffles' collection)

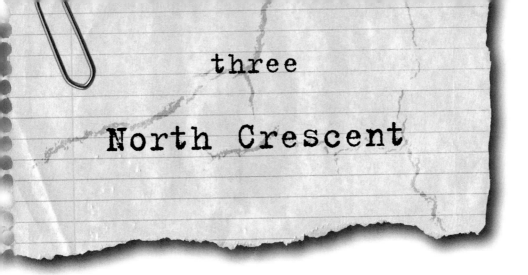

three

North Crescent

A House in North Crescent

Ghost dog

In the 1930s, Peter Fountain and his family lived in North Crescent. He remembers an odd incident which occurred when he was only about five years old. Peter says:

I used to occupy a small bedroom at the top of the staircase; I recollect the staircase went up and swung round to the right. I woke up one night and I could see flames and a dog, a big Alsatian, sitting framed in the door. I yelled blue murder. I think my father came in and calmed me down and after that I tended to sleep in one of the other rooms.

North Crescent. (Hertford Museum collection)

The room Peter is referring to is probably that with the big old fireplace above the dining room. Another resident who moved into the house after the Fountain family had vacated was Maisie Ditton. She felt that the ghost in the property was that of an animal.

Hertford Hospital

Caught on camera at Hertford Hospital

The ghost of a former nurse has been seen many times at Hertford Hospital. Staff have become so familiar with the phantom that they have named her Mabel. One evening, one of the staff was on duty when she heard a female voice call out 'Sister'. She immediately looked round but there was nobody there and she knew that only she and a male porter were in the building at the time.

Staff believe Mabel has been caught on the CCTV cameras on more than one occasion. One piece of footage shows a thick black cloud emerging from the lift, which moves to the front doors and then returns to the lift before floating back to the front doors and out into the corridor. Often the lift doors will open and close by themselves when no one is around, and there are many areas of the hospital which have inexplicable cold spots. At one time, an X-ray plate was developed which had the imprint of a hand on it, which shouldn't have been there.

The original hospital opened in 1833 as a general infirmary; a new building was constructed here in recent years and staff and patients have reported seeing Mabel walk through a wall where the old morgue was situated. But it seems Mabel is not the only ghost to haunt the hospital. One day, a member of staff was putting out linen in an area of the building occupied by Roche products. All the lights were off and the area had a particularly spooky feeling. She noticed a doctor in a white coat, but she later learned that no staff were in the area at the time and she had indeed been completely alone.

four

Old Cross

OLD Cross is the site of the former Saxon market place. Many graves have been found here as the area was once the churchyard for St Mary the Less, one of Hertford's lost churches, which began as a preaching cross with a cemetery surrounding it. Eventually the cross became purely a market cross, which stood here until the eighteenth century. St Mary the Less was pulled down in 1514. All that remains is a drinking fountain (this was constructed in 1890 from fragments discovered in the cellars of a big house, which was demolished to make way for the library). A settlement grew up here and houses were built along St Andrew Street

Old Cross fountain and memorial tablet. (Hertford Museum collection)

Old Cross. Remains of St Mary the Less were discovered in the cellars of an old house. (Hertford Museum collection)

and Cowbridge. The borough library and art school was opened in 1889, and the quaint little lane running alongside it once led to the house of a brewer whose Hope Brewery was incorporated into McMullens in 1920. The public library was moved in 2012 to its new location in Dolphin Yard.

Wigginton's

Wigginton's wraiths

The former Wigginton's store was a Hertford institution, trading for many years as a toy and gift shop in what is now Café Yum in Old Cross. When the late Roy Roberts took the shop on, customers browsing upstairs would come down and tell him that the building was haunted. He said, 'One lady went into the room above the toy shop, formerly the back bedroom, and said there was definitely a spirit there. Her husband later told me she was a psychic.'

Jane Holt, Roy's daughter, lived in the back bedroom until she was eighteen. As she lay in bed at night, a lady in Victorian clothes would often wake her by stroking her brow. Jane wasn't frightened as this lady seemed to bring a great feeling of love. A man with white hair and beard, dressed in a mourning suit, would also stand at the end of the bed.

Hertford School of Art, in the library building. (Hertford Museum collection)

Wigginton's. (Hertford Museum collection)

Former employees in the building were scared of going up to the room above the toy shop to make their tea because many of them had sensed a ghostly presence. The late Graham Wyley, psychic investigator, went in to see what he could do. He said, 'Immediately [when] I entered the haunted room, I went cold. This indicates there is a presence here.' Graham also experienced an oppressive feeling in his chest, which had been reported by some visitors to the shop on other occasions. Graham believed the room had originally been a bedroom when the building was constructed in the 1500s. 'There is a feeling of grief in the room. A young lady nursed her dying father here, hence Jane's experience of the hand across the brow.' The spirit in this room, Graham felt, was benevolent.

However, it was a different story in the attic storeroom of Wigginton's. Jane refused to go up there and dogs have behaved very strangely at the bottom of the stairs, growling and whining as if at an invisible intruder. Graham Wyley took up the case. 'There is something nasty and evil in this room,' he concluded, 'I can't wait to get out. I got a choking feeling in my throat as soon as I entered. I feel it was about 1750 and a young man, on the run for murder and feeling the net closing in around him, came up here to hang himself from one of the beams, thus cheating the gallows. It is the evilness of this man's actions for taking another's life that remains in this room.'

Next door is a health shop, where it appears the same Victorian lady floats in from Wigginton's, with a companion – a Victorian gentleman in high collar. Before the First World War the shop would have been considerably larger, as it was reduced when Mill Bridge was opened. The shop's proprietor also used to work at Mill House, and was aware of an unfriendly presence in a back room which was once the kitchen.

Sugar Hut

Gruesome goings-on

Late-night bar the Sugar Hut is situated at No. 11 Old Cross. A blood-soaked police-woman has been seen in a mirror, a blurred figure was captured on CCTV when the building was empty, and a cleaner heard the words 'Get out!' whispered aggressively in his ear early one morning.

This building was originally built around 1879 together with a coffee house. It was the Working Men's Club. Tinderbox Alley, which had stood here, was condemned following a cholera outbreak in 1848. In the last thirty years, various bars have occupied the site.

Ghost Hunter's Notes: The story of the police-woman in the mirror is interesting for two reasons. Firstly, the ghost is of someone presumably quite modern and certainly the most contemporary ghost in these stories. Although this is unusual it is not unheard of and poses the question as to why most ghosts seem to be of a time much further back than the last five years. The answer might be that ghosts that appear solid (due to being recently formed), and which are wearing modern fashions, simply go unnoticed. Secondly, the fact it was seen in a mirror is interesting. For countless years reflective materials such as glass, stone, crystal or water have been used for scrying – in other words to see the future, past or otherworldly events or beings. Could it be that the person who saw this ghost has innate psychic abilities?

No. 5

Stranger behind the curtain

In recent years, this property housed a clothes shop. Down in the basement, items of clothing would rise and fall by themselves on the rails as if caught by a sudden invisible breeze. Trainers would also move themselves from one side of the shop to the other. A dark shadow would be seen moving across the white downstairs wall from the upper floor, tobacco was mysteriously smelt, and something was heard moving about when there was no one downstairs.

Old Cross, showing No. 11 on the left as the Working Men's Club in the Temperance Hotel. (Hertford Museum collection)

Old Cross, showing No. 5 to the immediate left of the old post office archway. (Hertford Museum collection)

One day, a member of staff working downstairs in the shop saw someone walk towards a curtain which separated the sales area from the stockroom behind. She called to the stranger that it was a private area and, as they went behind the curtain, followed them into the stockroom. But the stranger had vanished into thin air. Another member of staff was so convinced she was being watched in the downstairs toilet that she stripped it out to ensure there was no camera concealed there! On finding nothing, she refused to use the toilet, preferring to cross to the pub opposite.

The proprietor was working into the early hours recently, decorating the shop ready for opening, when at about 2 a.m. he felt something which he describes as 'like a Jack Russell dog' jumping up his leg and clawing at it. When he looked down, there was nothing.

The top of the building is a flat and the occupants have experienced a sound described as like 'jellybeans being thrown onto lino'. The whole family heard this curious sound and found it very disturbing. They felt compelled to clean the floor to ensure nothing had been thrown down.

One day, a lady came into the shop and felt the atmosphere was so frightening that she offered to 'clear it'. The family vacated the building for a short while one Sunday whilst the lady performed her ritual and, on returning, they found the atmosphere was totally different, '… as if a wall had been removed, allowing cold air to blow all the way through and clear the building'. One of the things the lady had discovered was that the downstairs area had been full of children's spirits.

No. 5 Old Cross in its former role as an antique shop. (Peter Ruffles' collection)

five

Fore Street

DURING the 1600s and 1700s there were more coaching inns in Hertford than any other town in the county, it being a terminus for five coaches to London. Inns stood in a continuous line from the post office in Fore Street to the Blackbirds in Parliament Square. The main impression for a visitor wandering along Fore Street is of a succession of inns or former inns with their coaching arches, or wagon ways, leading to the yards behind. Some have been demolished, others adapted as restaurants or other businesses, but this has made no difference to the ghosts who continue to haunt the buildings.

Fore Street before Market Street was built, c. 1899. The statue of Ceres can clearly be seen atop the Corn Exchange. (Hertford Museum collection)

A more bustling Fore Street in 1921. On the immediate left is Neale's Bon Marche Ltd, which is now the much-haunted Prezzo restaurant. The building adjacent to the right of the Corn Exchange was demolished to make way for Market Street. (Hertford Museum collection)

Fore Street, at the entrance to Chequers Yard (now long gone), showing Savage's shop and the Talbot Arms, c. 1889. Dimsdale Arms at the edge of the photograph is now a Pizza Express. (Hertford Museum collection)

Rear of the Dimsdale Arms. The strangely empty space on the horizon was soon to be filled by the Gascoyne Way car park. (Peter Ruffles' collection)

This street, which was widened in the 1800s, once had a gaol, whipping post, cage and pillory. Behind the frontages of many of the buildings, their true history is revealed. Some have alleys and yards resembling a secret world that is unchanged – except for the gruesome concrete spectre of the Gascoyne Way multi-storey car park in the background! Don't forget to look up. You may even notice the stone owl atop Sheffield chemist.

Hertfordshire Mercury

Terrifying events at the Mercury

The paranormal reputation of the former *Hertfordshire Mercury* office building, now the Hertford House Hotel, is well known in Hertford. *Mercury* staff member Gary Matthews says, 'You talk to all the people who have worked here over the years and they will tell you about the strange noises and the presence that has been felt.' Gary was a sceptic himself, until one Christmas in the late 1990s when he happened to be working alone late one night.

> I suddenly became aware of the lights flashing on and off. I checked my computer screen and that was OK, so I knew it wasn't the power. Then I heard the door handle moving and when I looked over at the door, the handle was indeed moving up and down.

Gary looked around the building to check no one else was around playing tricks on him, but the building was empty. When he returned to his seat, the lights went off completely then came on again, and the door handle began moving once more. Gary hurriedly packed up and made a swift move home.

Mike Poultney was in the *Mercury* building one Sunday and was just locking up when he heard a door slam above him.

Thinking there must be an intruder, he called the police. An officer with a large black German shepherd came to search the premises and sent the dog into the cellar to ensure no one was hiding there. After a few minutes, the dog began desperately scratching at the door and shot out of the cellar, its hair standing up on end. Continuing the search of the rest of the building, they came to an office which had a bunch of keys in the lock. The keys were swinging round and round as if someone had just closed the door. Brandishing his truncheon, the policeman rushed into the room, but it was empty. It was the final straw and, with that, both policeman and dog made a hasty departure.

The cellar is reputedly haunted by a kitchen maid who was murdered by the butler sometime in the past. Also, a machine operator is reported to have died

The former Mercury offices in Fore Street, now Hertford House Hotel. (Hertford Museum collection)

there. Another former staff member at the *Mercury* reports that one day he saw the figure of a man walk through a solid wall.

Room 301 in the Hertford House Hotel is believed to be the former *Mercury* office where the police officer saw the keys swinging. Staff at the hotel have been asked by guests in Room 301 if they can be moved because they feel uneasy there. Other activity in the building includes doors slamming when rooms are empty; but it is the basement where strange events are still occurring most. This area is used as a communications room and is where the chefs change into their whites when coming on shift.

One morning at 6 a.m., member of staff Dannii Cutmore was just finishing her night shift and waiting for the kitchen staff to arrive. She was trying to fix a wireless internet problem which had occurred. In the semi-darkness of the room, Dannii saw what she describes as 'a brush-stroke of white light' which dashed in front of her from left to right. Then, French chef David came down to get changed at the start of his shift. They greeted each other and Dannii continued looking at the wireless router, when suddenly David let out a scream. Startled, she looked over and saw him standing with a leg outstretched as if something had got a grip on him. Dannii says, 'He was screaming out and I could see something tugging at his trouser material, like an invisible grip.' David managed to get away and the two of them ran upstairs and alerted the hotel manager, who dismissed the incident as simply David getting his trousers caught on something. But Dannii thought differently and so went back down to the basement, taking a torch with her, to examine the spot. But she could find no cause for what had happened. David never returned to the basement.

Pizza Express

Underground goings-on

Opposite the Corn Exchange, on Fore Street, once stood the Dimsdale Arms. This is now a Pizza Express restaurant. Before the inn was called the Dimsdale it was the Half Moon (*c.* 1726–1826), which had a grisly reputation because a highwayman was allegedly hanged from its inn sign in 1741. When the building was the Dimsdale, it was owned by McMullens brewery.

Andrew Newbury of McMullens brewery has been down in the cellars and tunnels beneath on brewery business on many occasions. When the Dimsdale Arms was being converted into Pizza Express, Andrew was working in the cellars and felt ghostly presences; he even saw colleagues run out because they experienced something unearthly. The restaurant has reported things being mysteriously moved and, during construction work, the builders were spooked on more than one occasion. Andrew has seen contractors, consultants and surveyors turn and leave the cellars because of the overpowering presences they have sensed and the overwhelming feeling of discomfort. Andrew has seen two passageways beneath Pizza Express, but they are now blocked off.

Ghost Hunter's Notes: Again tunnels are mentioned. Historians have questioned the existence of some of the tunnels and especially their connection with the Templars. These ones I myself have been privileged enough to see as part of an investigation into the existence of Knights Templar tunnels. I can confirm that the cellar beneath Pizza Express definitely has old tunnels that run in the direction of the church. They are low and brick-lined, and, although the tunnels looked old, the brickwork seemed to be no older than Tudor so these, at least, are not the hiding place of the Grail!

Dimsdale Arms, c. 1972. (Hertford Museum collection)

As far as ghostly activity, the feeling was oppressive there although, at the time, we were unaware of any stories associated with paranormal experiences and we presumed any feeling of unease was due to the dank air and claustrophobic surroundings.

Master's House

Playful spirit

Now a boutique hotel, bar and restaurant opened in 2009, this building was once the house of the Master of Hale's Grammar School. Although now torn apart by the Gascoyne Way relief road, the Master's House and the Grammar School were once on the same plot of land and could be reached via the long garden at the rear of the house. It may cause some surprise that the headmaster had such a large dwelling but, in order to supplement his income, it was usual for the head to take in private pupils who would live in the house.

The Master's House. (Hertford Museum collection)

In 2012, a succession of chefs working in the restaurant have walked out of their jobs because they say paranormal activity has made it unbearable to work there. One day, during a quiet spell, some of the staff began joking around and playing frisbee with the lid from an empty bucket of mayonnaise. Later in the evening, only two of the staff remained at work: one on duty in the bar, the other a chef in the kitchen. The chef was taking stock of the kitchen stores in preparation for an order when he was hit on the side of the head. When he looked down, the lid from the mayonnaise bucket was on the floor beside him. No one else was in the kitchen at the time. The other member of staff was working in the bar in a different part of the hotel. Was this a playful ghost who wanted to join the game? Perhaps the spirit was familiar with toys and games, as the Master's House was once a toy shop.

Threshers

A chilling feeling

Number 41 Fore Street has always had an association with the sale of alcohol. This building was part of an inn called the Cross Keys until 1861, and in 1866 a wine and spirit merchants was housed here and has been ever since.

The manageress of the former Threshers wine store reported a 'chilling feeling' in the cellar which made the hairs on the back of her neck stand on end. Frequently a tap would be found turned on fully with water pouring onto the floor when staff arrived for work in the morning – despite the building having stood empty overnight. One day, a tremendous crash was heard from the bottle store and, on investigation by staff, six bottles were found on the floor, neatly arranged in the shape of a star.

Fore Street, Threshers. (Hertford Museum collection)

According to the manageress, this was the scariest thing to have happened.

Ian from Hertford was in Threshers one day being served by an assistant. Suddenly, there came an almighty crashing sound from behind him. The metal shutters were shaking violently, but no one had touched them and there was no wind and no apparent reason for this occurrence. 'It's just the ghost,' said the assistant nonchalantly. 'Totally harmless, it happens quite often.'

It is recorded that when the Cross Keys was pulled down in 1861, 'a man was killed in the pulling down by his own inadvertence'. Perhaps it is his restless spirit that has haunted the building ever since. Moreover, below this building are the chambers from the former gaol which stood on the site now occupied by the Corn Exchange. The Corn Exchange has also had its share of hauntings, but more of that later.

Prezzo

The most malevolent haunting in Hertford? At 17-21 Fore Street, Prezzo restaurant can be found. This building's previous incarnations have included various eating establishments, a clothing emporium and a shoe shop. It is of late eighteenth-century origin with a modern shop front, rebuilt in the 1950s. Paranormal investigators have concluded that this is the most malevolent haunting in the town, and chilling reports tell of a strange half-man, half-beast believed to haunt the building. At one time it was a charity shop called the Stort Trust and the ladies who staffed the shop refused to use the toilets because they felt there was an evil atmosphere which made them uncomfortable. Instead, they would walk a fair distance across town to the public toilets in the Gascoyne Way car park.

During its transformation from charity shop to restaurant, the builders had many

Shire Hall, standing on the site of the old Sessions House and Neale's Bon Marche, now Prezzo. (Hertford Museum collection)

strange experiences – which they were initially reluctant to reveal. One particular week, some pieces of timber which had been left leaning against a wall suddenly moved across the room as if taken by unseen hands. This was witnessed by three of the men working on the site. The day before, some wires running across the ceiling had been mysteriously ripped out of the clips holding them in place and were left hanging danger-ously. During the building of the internal wall, bricks that had been left un-cemented in the wall in preparation for the next day were moved 90°. No explanation could be offered. The builders also witnessed an unearthly mist rising up from the basement and, one particular Christmas time at 2 a.m., the staff were cashing up when marching shadows began moving around the walls.

The toilets seem to again be a source of unease, with customers complaining of doors slamming violently of their own accord, as if aggressively shoved by an unseen hand. In recent years, one customer found herself locked in the toilet, which could only be locked from the inside, and had to climb over the top of the cubicle to get out. On examination, nothing wrong could be found with the locking mechanism. There is also a chandelier in the vicinity of the toilets, which continually sways.

One Sunday morning, after work on the restaurant had been completed, the cleaner was working alone up on the second floor. A chain ran across the top of the stairs to keep the public out. The cleaner replaced this chain as he began his work when sud-denly an almighty crash came from the floor below. 'It was a tremendous noise, like a lorry dropping off a skip,' he said. He rushed downstairs and, as he did so, noticed the chain had been removed. But even stranger, he could find no explanation as to the cause of the noise.

In the early 1700s, a cage, pillory and whipping post were all sited beside the Sessions House, where Shire Hall now stands, right next to the Prezzo building. With such grim history, perhaps it is no surprise that the echoes can still be felt in the vicinity.

The building's adjoining yard abuts the White Hart premises. The White Hart currently has its own troublesome spirit in the cellar. Perhaps the ghosts move seamlessly from building to building?

Ghost Hunter's Notes: This story of the beast in the upstairs corridor sounds very much like the haunting of an 'elemental'. A strange, fearful creature emanating feelings of malevolence and having an ability to physically manipulate objects is all very common in an elemental haunting. These energies seem to be protecting a site and are particularly active when the building is undergoing renovations. (For more information on types of ghost, *see* Endnote.)

Sheffield Chemist

The ghost with a story to tell
This charming old-fashioned shop has all the sights and smells of the traditional chemists of the past. One day in May 1996, the pharmacist reported a strange knocking sound on the floorboards upon which he stood. Wherever he tried to move to escape the knocking, it followed him. The following day a bottle of special diabetic medicine travelled along the passage by itself and smashed in front of witnesses, and then a shelf crashed to the floor. Pat Blake, a member of staff, said, 'I felt nervous at first, but as time went on, we got used to it. In fact, we used to talk to it in the end and it would respond with one knock for yes, two knocks for no.' But things were

Sheffield chemist, 1970s. (Hertford Museum collection)

to get stranger at Sheffield's. 'One day, a bottle of strychnine just appeared through the wall. It just came out of thin air and dropped to the floor without smashing,' said Pat. Strychnine may be classed as poison today, but it was used as a medicine in the past. The bottle was taken straight to the police. Pat continued:

Another time we found one of our 200-year-old prescription books somewhere it shouldn't have been. It was opened at a particular page and then the next day it just vanished. We hunted high and low for it, but it couldn't be found. So I asked out loud: 'Can we have our book back?' and about an hour later it literally appeared through the wall and fell to the floor with a bang. But the strangest thing was it was still open at the page it had been open at before. It was like it was trying to tell us something.

Sheffield's Victorian front and glass. (Peter Ruffles' collection)

Ghost Hunter's Notes: The materialisation of objects (also known as 'apports') such as mentioned in this story are extremely rare and must require a lot of energy to occur. One report of such an event was during a vigil in a haunted castle. A mist seemed to build in the centre of the circle and, with a clank, a metal goblet hit the floor from seemingly nowhere. One man rushed forward and picked it up only to find it extremely hot, causing him to drop it straight back down; he received a severe burn. This man still bears the scar as a reminder of this very strange experience. The goblet turned out to be from the castle and had moved from a neighbouring room.

Marshall's Furnishings

Face at the window

When Marshall's furnishings suffered a major fire in the warehouse store at the rear of the shop, four police officers were assigned for duty there on 30 September 1996. The warehouse was so badly damaged that the police had offered twenty-four-hour cover, as the building was virtually open and a prime target for looters.

It was the woman police constable who had the unenviable job of guarding the back of the building overnight. As she stood there alone in the windy darkness, glass was falling all around her from the heat-cracked windows above. On looking up, she saw a man peering from one of the upper window shells. It was no usual man. She described him as a 'Cromwellian figure' with long black curly hair and a moustache. The hairs on her neck bristled and she screamed down the radio for help. When her colleagues arrived, they went inside to search the hollowed building but could find nobody there. The WPC remains adamant to this day about what she saw.

Pat decided to contact the Society for Psychical Research, but the ghost had other ideas. Stamps disappeared and, when she tried to place a call, the phone went dead. 'One day I asked if it had a story to tell and it tapped out yes,' said Pat intriguingly. 'It told us by way of letters represented by taps that it had been killed by its brother in order to inherit the business.'

Its story told, the ghost seemed to quieten down, although a member of staff in recent years still feels a presence and says she can sense that a murder took place in the building. The building extends a long way and is extremely old. Tucked away in the back are boxes of fascinating old prescription books; some are over 200 years old. Sheffield's itself has been there since 1904. In the records, there is an intriguing note written in 1904 which simply says: 'he went abroad and his son died'.

Before the building of Gascoyne Way, a narrow passage existed between Sheffield's and No. 32, running directly to All Saints' churchyard.

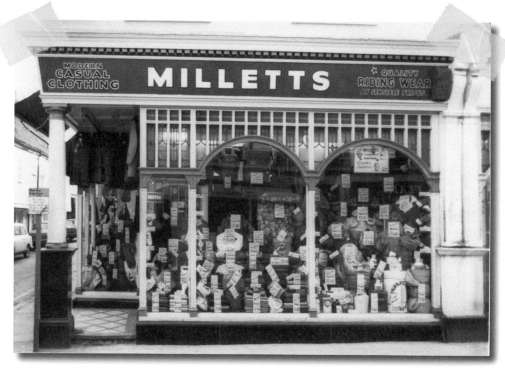

Milletts, 1970s. (Hertford Museum collection)

A tunnel was discovered in Bell Lane. Milletts is on the corner of this street – could the tunnel be connected to the paranormal activity? (Hertford Museum collection)

The King's Head, Bell Lane. Milletts occupies part of the building where this inn once stood. (Hertford Museum collection)

Salisbury Arms. (Hertford Museum collection)

A customer to the shop in 2000 had cause to visit the storeroom and asked if the building was haunted. She said she could sense a presence in the back. A psychic investigated the storehouse in October and picked up the spirit of a forty-six-year-old man, but, unfortunately, no further description was forthcoming.

Nearby, Milletts outdoor shop has something in the basement. This area is used as a stockroom and previous sales assistants have disliked going down there because of a feeling of unease. One girl was touched on the shoulder by an unseen hand. This building was the King's Head Inn between 1621 and 1719, after which it was converted into tenements.

Salisbury Arms Hotel

Secrets of the Salisbury
The charming Salisbury Arms in the centre of town has the ground plan of a medieval inn. One day, the cleaners were working up on the first floor when a middle-aged man dressed in black walked across the corridor and into a small room where the hot plate is kept. Thinking he was a lost guest, the cleaner went to investigate but found that the room was empty. There was no other exit; it appeared the visitor had completely

vanished. Also, various people at different times have seen a Cromwellian figure walking the corridor. Room 6 is said by staff to be the haunted bedroom.

The Salisbury was the Bell until 1820, named after the market bell which hung in Market Place. It was first recorded in 1431 and the date of 1570 above the doorway may refer to when the building first became an inn. The large gates in both Bell Lane and Church Street were wagon ways into the courtyard.

Ghost Hunter's Notes: The outside of the hotel clearly shows a 'SA' logo that probably stands for Salisbury Arms. The interesting thing about this, though, is that the 'A' is a set of compasses, a recognised Masonic symbol. The Salisbury Arms has been a meeting place for the Masons since 1829. Not that I believe this would have any bearing on the hauntings.

Corn Exchange

Phantom performances
Built during the nineteenth century, the Corn Exchange used to house musicals and shows and now has the reputation of being haunted. The caretaker, in recent

The first Corn Exchange, Fore Street, 1840. (Hertford Museum collection)

years, would go in during the day when the building was empty and hear scenery shifting, musicians clearing their throats and instruments being tuned, but there would be nobody there. In 2007 the manager took a photograph in the bar area and a mysterious shadowy shape appeared in the shot, though he was completely alone in the building.

The ladies' toilet has a malevolent feeling and this has been sensed by many psychics who have come for Psychic Evening events organised at the venue. Additionally, the manager heard a crowd of people talking in the men's toilet on one occasion when the building was closed. When he went in to investigate, there was no one there. The jangle of keys and the pulley mechanism, which operates the curtain, have also been heard when the building is empty.

Between 1702 and 1775 the County Gaol stood on the site that is now the Corn Exchange. Overcrowding, filth and lack of air made it a constant menace to the town. There were several outbreaks of smallpox and cholera, and hangings would take place outside. It was in a continual state of filth, disrepair and had no ventilation. It was only in 1777 that a new prison was constructed along Ware Road. After the closure of the gaol, the area became a butchers' market and a covered vegetable and meat market. In the 1850s a Corn Exchange was established here, complete with a statue of Ceres, the corn goddess, atop the roof. Ceres' head can now be found in Hertford Museum. The Corn Exchange was sandwiched between two inns: the Cross Keys to the east, and to the west the George (formerly the Swan), which occupied part of Market Street.

In 1884 workmen putting in new drains in Fore Street uncovered some old foundations or walls in the middle of the street where the old gaol was thought to be.

Ghost Hunter's Notes: Phantom noises are the most commonly experienced form of paranormal occurrence. This may be due to noises requiring less energy than apparitions. Alternatively, if the stone tape theory is to be believed, the reason could be that it is more common, or more simple, for sounds to be recorded in the magnetic stone than visions. For more information on the stone tape theory, *see* Endnote.

Baroosh

Victorian in the vaults
Number 78 Fore Street is now a trendy bar/restaurant, but up until the mid-1990s Barclays Bank was housed here. One evening, at 5.30 p.m., a member of staff was locking up in the bank vault at Barclays when she felt something brush against her shoulder. When she turned around, she saw a lady in a Victorian outfit walk past. When the building was being converted from Barclays Bank to Baroosh, builders were unnerved by things continually being moved about.

This building has been much altered over time. An extra storey and a Regency front have been added to an earlier wooden-framed structure. At the turn of the century, the ground floor was a shop called Rayment and a recent examination suggested that the left-hand section was once part of the Dimsdale Arms, which originally stood next door. Samuel Stone, one of the Pilgrim Fathers who founded Hartford, Connecticut, once lived in a house which formed the middle section of this present building.

Barclays Bank, now Baroosh. (Hertford Museum collection)

Henry Rayment's shop. (Hertford Museum collection)

The Ram, 1970s. (Hertford Museum collection)

Albany Radio

Cupboard Hall

This building at 63-65 Fore Street was a private dwelling in Georgian times, charmingly named Cupboard Hall. One of former resident Susan Brown's earliest memories was of waking suddenly in the middle of the night: 'I saw a lady leaning over me at the foot of my bed. She wore a dress of very rich texture.' The lady was dressed in Georgian costume, suggesting she may have been one of the first residents of the building.

The Ram

'A disorderly victualling house'

In the latter part of 2011 and into 2012, new managers at the Ram public house have experienced strange goings-on in this old coaching inn. Doors will open and close by themselves and shapes have been seen flitting around the bar area. The upper floor has rooms which are available for bed and breakfast, but Room 1 is very hard to let.

It seems that no one feels very comfortable here and people choose not to stay in this particular room. Curiously, people have reported the distinct taste of blood in the mouth when in this area. Generally, it has been said there is an unpleasant atmosphere lingering here.

The Ram has a chequered history. In a survey of 1621, it was recorded as being a 'disorderly victualling house'. It changed its name to the Golden Lion in 1719 then back to the Ram in 1775. In 1832, during borough election disturbances, gangs of Whig and Tory supporters clashed in the vicinity. The Whigs took refuge in the Ram and Tory 'bullies' attempted to demolish the house, causing the landlord to fire a shot from an upper window. He was charged with attempted murder.

Red House

Still on duty

Further along Fore Street, at No. 119, stands the majestic Red House (thought to have been built in the mid-1700s) which became part of Christ's Hospital for the orphaned children of London in the late nineteenth century. A number of sightings of a lady dressed in a grey matron's outfit and carrying a tray up the stairs have been reported here. Perhaps she is one of the former members of staff employed to care for the children, reluctant to leave her duties.

Now housing different businesses, this building was the brewer's house in 1754. The former brewery was to the rear. Young's Brewery was situated here from 1754 to 1893, and Pryor, Reid & Co. brewed from 1893 to 1897. The buildings, including the Red House, were incorporated into the adjoining Bluecoat School from 1897.

An interesting historical fact is that between the Red House and Christ's Hospital building was once a little passage variously named Three Turns Lane, Meeting House Lane and Brewhouse Lane (one of two in the town), which was closed off in 1897. Nothing remains of this little lane today, except a tell-tale crack in the adjoining wall.

The Red House. (Hertford Museum collection)

Brewhouse Lane (no longer in existence), beside the Red House. (Hertford Museum collection)

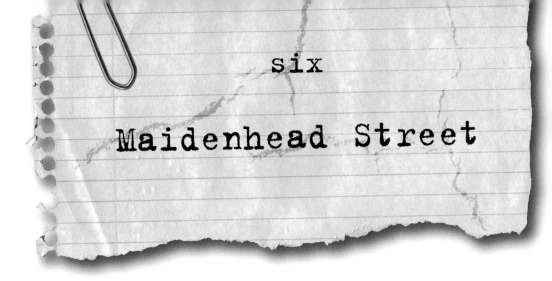

six

Maidenhead Street

BEFORE pedestrianisation, this street was choked up with passing traffic. It had various former names, including Back Street, Sowter Street and Cordwayner Street, but became Maidenhead Street around 1766 after the Maidenhead Inn which was built in the seventeenth century. The inn was demolished in 1931.

Fine Fare supermarket, c. 1970. (Hertford Museum collection)

Fine Fare

Ghosts in the machine

In the late 1970s, my next ghost story informant, Ian, worked at Fine Fare in Maidenhead Street. This building later became a McDonald's and, after remaining empty for some time, is now attached to Boots Opticians.

Ian worked at Fine Fare for eight years in total and, during that time, he experienced many strange things. For instance, a lift would take itself up to the first floor without being called. This lift could only have been called up by Ian or by someone actually inside the lift. The doors were heavy and manually operated so it could not have been someone pushing the button down-

stairs and then jumping out. In the same room, a rubbish baler, which was operated by a large manual lever, operated itself. A warehouse on the top floor was always intensely cold, and some staff would run out of the room as they felt suffocated by a heavy, unpleasant atmosphere.

One assistant manager was working late one evening but only managed twenty minutes on his own before being spooked out of the building. On another occasion, Ian was locking up the top floor around 8 p.m. on a Friday night. He went into the staff canteen and noticed an object left on a table by one of the staff. After going over to the other end of the room to unplug the kettle, he turned and froze on the spot. The object had moved off the table onto the window sill. Ian looked around the room, expecting someone to laugh and for the joke to be revealed, but chillingly the room was empty. Some moments later, his manager entered the room and, on seeing Ian, asked him if everything was OK. On being told what had just happened, he laughed and pulled Ian's leg about working too hard. A moment after that, one of the Saturday staff came in to ask the manager for some keys to the large padlock so he could chain the fire exit door. Once again the manager laughed and asked if he was the butt of Friday evening jokes as he had only just locked the padlock himself on the way to the staff canteen. The three of them went back downstairs and saw the large fire exit chain swinging loose. The manager abruptly stopped laughing. This door backed directly onto the then *Mercury* newspaper offices, also renowned for their paranormal activity. One of the butchers who had been on the staff for several years told Ian that older members of staff had named the ghost 'Godfrey' and that a man had once hanged himself from the stairs in the building.

On an interesting historical note, just behind the building is Evron Place shopping arcade (named after Hertford's twin town in France), which was constructed in the late 1970s. During the digging work, a number of skeletons were unearthed. Ian watched them being retrieved from the staffroom window. Skeletons were also uncovered in Market Square in 1975 during sewer replacements. These bones were dated by British Museum anthropologists to the late Saxon period, around 900–1066. Archaeologists say it was not unusual for the outskirts of early market places to be used for the interment of bodies.

Old Maidenhead Inn, 1886. (Hertford Museum collection)

Ghost Hunter's Notes: Could this be the location of an ancient burial site? This could certainly explain the hauntings in Monsoon (*see* Chapter Seven) and it is only a stone's throw away from Prezzo, the building haunted by the 'half-man half-beast'. This strengthens the argument that the entity may be an 'elemental' (*see* Endnote).

The former Woolworths store (now Pound Stretcher) in Maidenhead Street stands on the site of an old pub called the Maidenhead. Three members of staff had strange experiences in the Woolworths storeroom, which was situated above the audio section, accessed by a staircase. A heavy 6ft-long clothes rail moved by itself and clothes were unaccountably thrown around. Former shop assistant Gwen Busson tells of how one day a cage followed a girl down the aisle. Other staff report that some assistants were afraid to go into the stockroom.

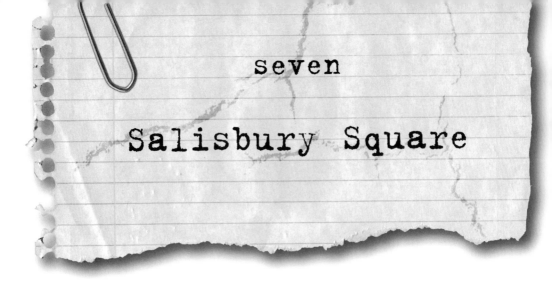

seven

Salisbury Square

White Hart

Mischievous spirit

The cellar of the White Hart is haunted by a mischievous spirit that moves stock around. The White Hart is the only pub in Hertford to have had the same name for nearly 400 years. The building is much altered and the present façade is thought to include oak timbers taken from the Sessions House which was demolished prior to the construction of the present Shire Hall. In a survey of Hertford in 1621, the White Hart was recorded as having three cottages attached and was held by Sampson Clarke, gaoler at Hertford Gaol from 1628.

The White Hart Hotel, Salisbury Square, c. 1972. (Hertford Museum collection)

Monsoon

Phantom footsteps

A *Guardian* reporter visited Monsoon in Hertford Market Place in 2005, enquiring about the rumours of a tunnel beneath the shop and its connection with the Knights Templar in Hertford. He was unsuccessful in his quest to find a tunnel, but he did discover that the shop is 'definitely haunted'. During sales meetings, footsteps can be heard overhead when the shop is closed and empty.

This building was Hertford's well-known Gravesons department store for many years, and the area occupied by Monsoon would, in the late 1800s, have been the living quarters for the family of Samuel Graveson, including his seven children. When work was being done to turn the upstairs into rented properties, the builders described the place as 'an absolute rabbit warren'.

Ghost Hunter's Notes: Templars once more! From my experiences in Hertford's tunnels, the majority of them seem to date from the Tudor period and are not as old as the Templar dissolution in 1306. These tunnels would probably have been extended cellars that may all have linked at one time, but most I know of are now bricked up for security reasons. There may be tunnels from other time periods in Hertford; for instance, there are rumours of a tunnel constructed for the purposes of enabling a secret society to meet, leading from Bailey Hall to the building that now houses the Lussmanns restaurant.

Gravesons and the Flower Pot inn (right), c. 1972. (Hertford Museum collection)

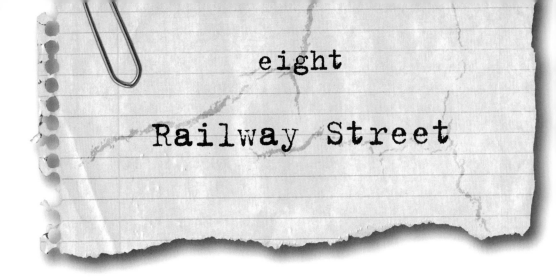

eight

Railway Street

RAILWAY Street was so named in 1844 because it was the most direct route through the town to Hertford's first railway station. The street was previously Back Street. A recruitment agency on the street has complained of mysterious footsteps running up and down their stairs and, on investigation by staff,

Railway Street as it was. These buildings have long since been removed. (Hertford Museum collection)

no one has been found to account for the noise.

Nos 23-25

Creepy cellar

These premises, in a one-time rough and deprived area of the town, boast the phantom smell of tobacco down in the cellar. The building was previously owned by Pearce's Bakers. At the time, staff member Sheila Woodford said, 'We're not allowed to smoke down there yet there's the distinct smell of cigars sometimes. I get a cold shiver when I have to go down there, it gives me the creeps.' Pictures were reported to fall off the counter for no reason and objects flew off the shelves when no one was nearby. At the time of writing the property is empty, but it has most recently been a furniture shop.

Railway Street, c. 1972. J. Wren & Sons bakery was later to become the haunted Pearce's Bakers. Notice the covered market before its demolition. (Hertford Museum collection)

No. 12

Someone's up there!

Wallie's butchers (which became 'John's') occupied No. 12 until around 2002. In the 1960s a couple moved into the flat above the shop. Pat and Ted Robinson had come to Hertford from London because Ted had a brother living here and, being a butcher, Ted was able to get a job at the shop.

Wallie's butchers, Railway Street, 1972. (Peter Ruffles' collection)

When they first moved in, Ted began hearing a baby cry at exactly 10 p.m. every night. There were no neighbours and nobody was about. The building had three storeys and he rushed upstairs to see if their children were all right. They were sound asleep. After a couple of weeks, Ted and Pat got used to the sound and took no notice of it. But then, one night, they were in bed when suddenly a noise like a solid three-wheeled bike riding on bare boards could be heard from the attic. Frightened out of their wits, Pat said to Ted, 'You've got to go up and look. Someone's up there.' Together, the couple plucked up the courage to venture up the stairs to the attic, but, as soon as Ted opened the door, the noise stopped immediately. Ted says, 'I looked all around. Nothing; nothing about at all. But in the old days it was an inn and soldiers used to sleep in the loft.'

Between 1857 and 1919 an inn called the Black Horse occupied No. 12 Railway Street and, in recent years, many retailers have come and gone. None seem able to remain for more than a few months.

Opticians

Spectres of Specsavers

Just around the corner from Railway Street is Bircherley Green Shopping Centre, constructed in 1983. One of the shops in this precinct is Specsavers. Voices have been heard upstairs in the dispensing room, in particular a man's voice. The figure of a man has also been seen walking around. Dark shadows have been witnessed flitting about and staff have been called by name when there is no one there. One member of staff sneezed when she was alone in the room and a voice from nowhere said, 'Bless you.' Downstairs,

Butcherly Street, now the site of Bircherley Green Shopping Centre. The houses were pulled down in 1891. (Hertford Museum collection)

each member of staff has their own desk and, one morning in 2012, one employee came into work to find her desk a complete mess. Items had been thrown around and all the glasses moved. The spirit isn't thought to be malevolent and seems to be particularly active during periods of change.

This area was formerly Butcherly Green, a poverty-stricken slum area of courts, yards and alleys. It was densely populated, very rundown and riddled with disease. Open sewers discharged into the river, and drunkenness and violence were common. Built in the nineteenth century, tumbledown weather-boarded buildings were cramped in on top of each other. Pubs on Butcherly Green included the City Arms, the Bricklayers Arms and the Butchers Arms. There was also the Ragged School, which opened in 1859, providing education for poor children. The dwellings were finally demolished in the 1920s. Locals called it 'The Green' and it is now the site of the shopping centre and bus station. It also stretched alongside the river, where there is now a smart residential development.

Bircherley Green Shopping Centre, c. 1982. (Hertford Museum collection)

Where the slums had stood. Bircherley Green Shopping Centre under construction, 1980. (Hertford Museum collection)

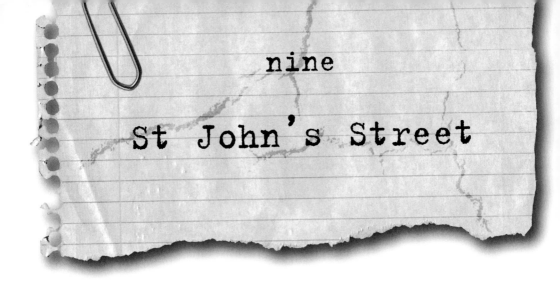

nine

St John's Street

Unnamed Flat

Phantom in the flat

This story was related by David, a Hertford resident who occupied a flat above a funeral director's in St John's Street near the Hertford East station. David would be working on his computer and see, out of the corner of his eye, a dark shape the size of a man drift past the open door and disappear through the bathroom wall. Food in the house would go off very quickly; fruit would last less than a couple of days and the same with bread. It would often be very cold in the flat. On one occasion, in the middle of the night, a fitted cupboard door in the bedroom flew open against the wall. Woken with a start, David collected himself and went to investigate. Nothing had fallen against the door and it closed again easily. There seemed to be no explanation for the violent action.

One night, a friend of David's came over to the flat for a meal and drinks. At the end of the evening, he said, 'Do you want to know?' David asked what about and he replied, 'Your ghost.' They had not spoken about anything David had experienced in the flat but his friend told him that there was a man who sometimes walked across the corridor in labourer's clothing, looking like he was from the early 1900s. He thought that this chap had lived in the building originally and would have worked downstairs, fixing or making something.

During the building of the residential area of nearby Mitre Court, many early medieval corpses were excavated and removed to Hertford Cemetery. Further down the street is a surprising little oasis amidst the Victorian cottages. The Immaculate Conception and St Joseph Catholic Church is tucked away with a peaceful courtyard, water feature and shady little cemetery. Built in 1858, a plaque on the wall of this church states that this was formerly the site of the Benedictine Hertford Priory, founded in 1087.

Ghost Hunter's Notes: This is an example of a replay ghost; passing through walls is the give-away. The walls of a building might have been in different places at the time a ghost was alive. In this case the wall locations are known to have changed, as the upper floor of this building was only recently converted into two separate flats. The plans clearly show that the bathroom wall is a new addition.

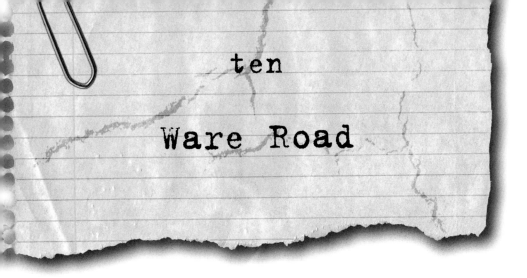

ten

Ware Road

Care Home

Restless residents

A support worker, employed by a service caring for people with learning difficulties, has experienced many things that he cannot explain. In this house, staff work a twenty-four-hour shift pattern, starting at 3 p.m. and ending at 3 p.m. the next day, therefore they are required to sleep overnight in the centre. Staff are allocated sleep time between 10.30 p.m. and 7 a.m. but are expected to be on call should the need arise. For one worker, sleep is not an option.

Working at least two sleep-ins per week, he has been woken many times by strange footsteps walking up and down the hallway, voices calling his name, knocking on the door and unexplained screaming. One night he was sleeping in a locked room when the duvet was suddenly yanked off him. He is not the only one to have experienced such strange activity; his colleagues have been subjected to similar events.

The centre is located in a large Victorian house a few doors down from the Saracen's Head pub on Ware Road. The house was built in 1870 and was formerly known as Oak Lodge. It stands well back from the road, behind a hedge, and its original five bedrooms, two toilets, entrance hall, dining, drawing and morning rooms have been converted to provide accommodation for six people with learning disabilities. The residents have limited mobility; once they are in bed, they do not stir.

Ware Road, 1900s. (Hertford Museum collection)

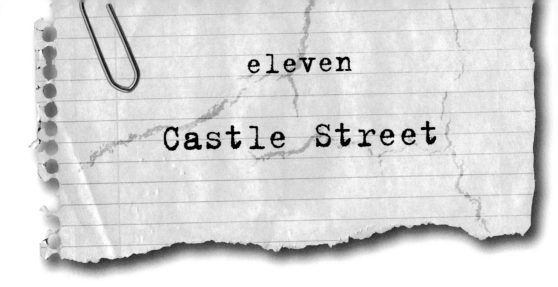

eleven

Castle Street

Hertford Castle

Night visitor

One would assume that an historic place such as Hertford Castle would be overflowing with past inhabitants, but surprisingly very little has been documented. Weedon Grossmith, famous for co-writing *The Diary of a Nobody*, stayed at the castle on several occasions but was never disturbed and 'never slept better than within its thick walls with the small Gothic windows'. However, one night he heard a thump at the door which woke him with a great start. He opened the door expecting to see Jock the fox terrier who lived at

Hertford Castle, 1900s. (Hertford Museum collection)

the castle, but the corridor was empty; just the gas jets burning, lighting up the passage beyond. Grossmith returned to bed, but five minutes later he heard another tremendous thump. This time he stayed in bed and could not fall asleep until daybreak. At breakfast he told Mrs Lowe, who rented the castle, of the nocturnal disturbances. She was unsurprised and told Grossmith that had he looked out of the window after hearing the thump he would have seen a little figure of a man crossing the lawn. She added, 'He seems to glide, and he carries what looks like a large apple in his hand.'

Around 1930 a Hertford man was returning from a dance. As he walked through the castle grounds he saw a hooded figure walking across the lawn. He said:

> It was bright moonlight so there was no question of the shadows playing tricks on me. The figure was carrying a large object like a family bible. As the figure disappeared behind a shrubbery it gave a blood curdling cry! I didn't stop to investigate. I ran all the way home.

Now council buildings, a former mayor reported that lights would go on and off mysteriously and a dog could be heard barking in the building, although no dog was ever discovered. During a Hertford Council committee meeting at the castle in 1920, unexplained tapping was reportedly heard in the room.

Ghost Hunter's Notes: Gliding ghosts can be explained by considering that they may just be the replay of a past event. The ground level was likely to be lower in the time this ghost actually walked the earth. Now the ground is higher but the replay is at the same level, so the feet are below ground level – hence the steps are masked by the earth (especially if the entity is wearing a robe or long skirt) and the entity appears to glide.

White Horse Inn

Spirits at the inn

The White Horse, with its unspoilt timbered upstairs and separate rooms, is sixteenth-century Grade II listed. Landlords here have experienced ghostly activity, with footsteps heard on the boards upstairs after closing and taps on the barrels being turned off.

twelve

West Street

WEST Street has been called the Way of Kings due to it being the route royalty took on their way to the castle. They would turn down what is now the dirt track to the football club en route to the royal hunting ground of Hertingfordbury Park. The street's importance grew with the castle. Only in the last half of the twentieth century did West Street become entirely residential.

Traditionally there was a mixture of commercial and industrial properties, such as Nicholls Brewery, the collar factory and private housing. The street's present extent is very much what it was 400 years ago, running westwards from the castle to the land belonging to Bridgeman House (No. 37) on one side and to Westfield on the other.

Before the construction of the Gascoyne Way in the 1960s, West Street and Castle

West Street, 1900s. (Hertford Museum collection)

West Street at night, looking west, c. 1960. (Hertford Museum collection)

Street were seamlessly adjoined. Numbers 20 and 22 were described in 1621 as being in 'Castle Street or West Street', as if the names were interchangeable. The Andrews and Wren map of 1766 shows West Street beginning near the Black Horse, and Westfield (No. 52) has sometimes been located at 'the west end of Castle Street'.

One of the houses in this street has the reputation of being haunted. A bell would ring on its own, and a little boy who lived here would never go down to the basement as he once saw an old woman down there whom he didn't know.

The Maltings

Ghost of No. 1

As you enter West Street from the relief road, the first building on the right is The Maltings, which was originally Brewery House and part of Nicholls Brewery, beside the river Lea which runs along the rear of the buildings. The business closed in 1965 with the coming of the relief road. Brewery House dated from 1719 and was converted to a hostel around 1970. The archway led to the brewhouse and a range of barns and stores. This area is now a series of dwellings named Westall Mews and it is at No. 1 that a resident experienced ghostly activity on many occasions.

Bridgeman House

Troubled souls

This is now divided into two properties, 37a and 37b. It has been troubled by a variety of hauntings. There are stories of a fair-haired child who opens and closes doors and runs along the landing in 37b

The family from No. 83 St Andrew Street play in 'their street', the newly built Gascoyne Way, May 1967. (Peter Ruffles' collection)

before disappearing through the partition dividing the property. In the early 1980s, the boy appeared when Victorian panelling was being removed from the ancient fireplace in 37b, then again one winter's evening when the occupant, John Porter, was returning home. He unlatched the garden gate and looked up to see a child's face at an upstairs window. Once the house had undergone an exorcism, the spectral child was seen no more.

Next door at 37a the residents, who were sensitive to spirit activity, sensed three trapped souls that were unable to pass to the other side. One of them has a long face and a moustache and 'struts around, his head in the air, looking every bit the lord of the manor'. It has been suggested that this is the ghost of William Frampton Andrews (1839–1918), a prominent Hertford businessman and co-founder of Hertford Museum. Andrews lived at No. 27 West Street and owned Bridgeman House in 1890.

Another spirit is thought to be Emma Devonshire, a long-time housekeeper at the property, who is seen dressed in a long black skirt and blouse with a white pinafore and her white hair tied in a bun. She is an angry spirit who slams doors and makes pictures and mirrors fall from walls. She is heard to wail, 'My beautiful house! What are you doing to my beautiful house?'

Front view of No. 37 West Street, Bridgeman House. (Hertford Museum collection)

Charles Bridgeman, unmarried, lived alone except for Emma, his resident housekeeper, for over forty years. The current family sense that no woman has ever been happy in this house.

The final ghost is that of a young woman called Mary, Marie or Maria. Steve Arscott was resident of the property in 2002 and, one day in December, he was drawn to a back bedroom by the sound of a woman weeping. There he found a distraught young woman who told him that she had become pregnant when unmarried. Her father had imprisoned her in the room for bringing shame on the family name. Tragically, both she and her baby died during childbirth on Christmas Eve. Records show that an Anna Maria Bridgeman died on 31 October 1791 aged seventeen, and, whilst she seems the most likely candidate for the haunting, the dates do not match. However, on 21 December 1791, seven weeks after Anna Maria's burial, her parents presented a child for baptism: William James Alexander. They named themselves as parents but one could speculate that this was the son of the ill-fated Anna Maria. The child died soon after baptism.

Bridgeman House was listed in the Schedule for Listed Buildings as being built in 1649, but it may in fact be older as a document of 1622 mentions it as a 'new built brick tenement'. The property was sold to R.T. and W.F. Andrews in 1890 for £525. The house is named after the Bridgeman family, one of whom, Charles (born in 1778), was organist at All Saints' Church for eighty-one years (between 1791 and 1873), earning him the accolade of the world's longest-serving organist. In 1841 he and his Glee Society group sang for Queen Victoria and Prince Albert at nearby Panshanger.

thirteen

Cowbridge

HE name Cowbridge evolved from where cattle were driven over the bridge on their way to the market. Cowbridge House was demolished to build the large houses that are now opposite the church. An old barn had been allowed to deteriorate on the spot where the new development stands, but it was taken down to make room for the houses.

The Cowbridge area is also famous as the one-time home of Biggles creator W.E. Johns. William Earl Johns was born in 1893 in nearby Bengeo but, while he was still young, the family moved into No. 41 Cowbridge, where his father was a tailor. Biggles became one of the most popular children's heroes ever.

New Flat

Horse ghost

A young mother occupying one of the new flats in the Cowbridge area was disturbed when her four-year-old son began complaining of seeing a horse in his modern bedroom. He was so adamant and frightened that she went to the local archives to find out what building had stood on the site prior to the flats. Research revealed that prior to 1950 there had indeed been a knacker's yard in the near vicinity. An old man was also seen in the flat. Another resident in the new development had experienced strange noises in the night and heard mysterious scratching at the windows.

Cowbridge House. (Hertford Museum collection)

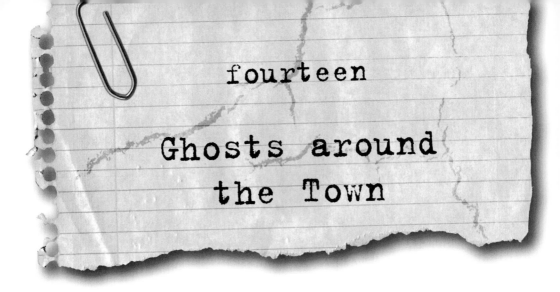

fourteen

Ghosts around the Town

Fore Street and County Hall

Invisible friend

In Fore Street, in a property above a shop opposite the Ram Inn, a local woman had to call in the assistance of a clairvoyant to help her discover what was haunting her young daughter. The four year old talked of her invisible friend and her behaviour began changing in a way that concerned her mother enough to seek specialist help.

This same Hertford woman was sitting outside the banqueting suite at County Hall when she heard someone calling her name. On looking round she could see no one and there wasn't anyone nearby who could be responsible.

Ghost Hunter's Notes: I have long held the belief that children's imaginary friends may be more than imaginary. I feel that children might be more sensitive to paranormal activity as they have yet to learn from society that this stuff isn't supposed to exist. As we grow up we pay less attention to things less physical and get more interested in belongings. It is thought that our senses take in so much infor-mation that our brains can only process part of it. The theory states that part of our brain called the reticular activating system (RAS) is responsible for deciding what is important for us to pay attention to; as we grow older ghosts become less important, so that information gets filtered out.

Cannons Gym

Weird old crone

Ian from Hertford reports that he once met a ghostly woman outside his gym at dusk. He describes her as 'a weirdly dressed old crone who looked like something out of a Brontë novel'. She fixed him with a gimlet eye and said, 'You'll be fine. It will all be fine.' Ian felt utterly mystified by the strange encounter. A few days later he was rushed to Harefield Hospital with heart failure and had to undergo a major opera-tion which proved to be touch and go. However, he fully recovered and lived to tell his strange tale.

Dicker Mill

Ghost of poor Doris

Dicker Mill, now long defunct, once housed DAG Engineering, makers of tea-vending machines and equipment. One of the ladies who worked on the fly presses was Doris Thrustle. Doris, who was in her mid-fifties, was described as a 'game girl'; the life and soul of any party. One day she had gone home complaining of a headache and never returned: she had died of a brain tumour.

At 2 a.m. on a hot summer night, late-shift workers at Dicker Mill saw Doris's ghost appear back at her fly press. The paint shop was up one end of the factory, the press works were at the opposite end, and the toilets were in the middle. Alfie Cobbman came out of the paint shop to go to the toilet and, on sliding the paint shop door open, saw Doris working her press. It was the morning of her funeral. Alfie shouted to his colleagues and they all saw Doris. After this experience, no one could be enticed to work nights any later than 10 p.m.

The factory has been described as a very creepy place, bitterly cold by the river and infested with rats. Today the area is a sprawling industrial estate at the Mead Lane end of town. There is a spooky rundown feeling to the site, which is currently mostly the haunt of auto-repair works.

The Old Vicarage

Romans at the gate

The Old Vicarage building can be found on Church Street and was formerly an osteopath's business. A patient visiting the clinic announced that she had seen two Roman centurions guarding the front gate when she came in. Also, a lady dressed in Victorian clothing has been seen walking across the

The Old Vicarage, 1930s. (Hertford Museum collection)

Church Street from All Saints' Church tower – before the Gascoyne Way sliced Hertford in two, c. 1964. (Hertford Museum collection)

When Church Street met All Saints' Church. (Hertford Museum collection)

entrance hall or loitering in the waiting area. The odd thing about this ghost is that she is only visible from the knees upwards, as is the case with many spirits, indicating changes in floor level over the centuries.

The vicarage is an historical property with the unusual feature of having the garden path made out of gravestones from the All Saints' Church across the dual carriageway.

Marshgate Drive

House of horrors

To the north-east of the town centre is Marshgate Drive. A row of Victorian cottages line one side of the street; they were once houses for the workers at the former gasworks, which stood nearby. The very end cottage in the terrace has been described as 'a house of horror' for Dannii Cutmore, who shared this rented property in 2001.

When she first moved in, Dannii's dad came round to help her put some items into the loft. He got halfway into the hatch before abandoning the idea and coming back down, saying there was something oppressive up there and he felt he could not go any further. Fellow tenants heard footsteps on the stairs when the house was otherwise empty, doors would slam by themselves, and Dannii had the feeling of being watched, particularly when she was in the shower.

Dannii's room was on the first floor and it was up here that most of the activity seemed to occur. Electrical items would misbehave and the volume on her stereo would suddenly turn itself up to maximum. Looking into the mirror in the en suite bathroom made her particularly uncomfortable, as she felt that she may see another face appearing behind her.

Things came to a head one night when a friend was staying over. Although the house is on the edge of a factory area, at night it is very quiet. After they had said goodnight, they both experienced the sound of extreme heavy breathing or 'huffing' coming towards them, getting louder and louder. The noise seemingly started from the direction of the fireplace and moved closer to them. It got inches from Dannii's face and she pulled the duvet up over her head and shouted to whatever it was to go away. The noise then moved in the direction of the en suite. The friends turned on the lights and sat bolt upright, shaking with fear. They ran out of the house and spent the rest of the night in the car, too frightened to go back inside. This was the final straw for Dannii and she gave up her tenancy immediately. Dannii did not go back to the house until March 2012. It was a sunny spring day, but just standing outside the dark little end-of-terrace property caused her visible fear and distress.

This area was known as Gas House Lane until 1969 when the residents asked for the street to be renamed. Gas House Lane was primarily an industrial area, named after the gasworks in 1825. Further along, at the end of today's Mead Lane, was the sewage works, and prior to that the area was mainly gravel pits.

Ghost Hunter's Notes: The 'face appearing in the mirror' entity has become a popular scene to include in recent horror movies – maybe this had coloured this person's view of what to expect in a spooky environment. This archetypal fear, though, probably dates back to superstitions of old, when it was thought that mirrors were able to trap a person's soul. Mirrors were also thought to be a tool used by witches for seeing spirits or the future.

Gallows Hill

Souls of the hanged

Residents on the Foxholes estate in the road named The Elms, on Gallows Hill, have seen phantoms wandering around at night. Are these the souls of those hanged at the gallows? The gruesomely named Gallows Hill, the location of public executions until 1812, has the reputation of being haunted by the sound of clanking chains and raised voices. A figure in grey loiters there. Perhaps this is the ghostly re-enactment of a condemned man's last journey, pursued by the angry mob.

In addition, at an undisclosed address on the Pinehurst estate, a modern house exuded an air of cold in a particular spot in the drawing room. The occupier called in a ghost investigator, who said she could see a woman in grey with two children in the corner of the room, walking slightly above floor level as if they were going uphill. Another householder in the same

Port Hill, showing the Reindeer Inn. (Hertford Museum collection)

area has experienced electrical problems and a shadow regularly appearing in the house. It was thought that the cold spot was over the route taken by condemned people from the old Hertford Gaol to the gallows at the top of Gallows Hill. However, this seems unlikely as the maps show the Pinehurst estate is too far east along the Ware Road to have been on the procession route of the condemned prisoner. Therefore whatever haunts this modern house remains a mystery.

Port Hill

Quaker wraith

One afternoon, a lady was walking along Port Hill with her daughter. As a young man walked towards her, she moved to one side to let him pass, but when she looked around he had disappeared. Thinking this a little odd, she voiced her surprise to her daughter, who claimed not to have seen anyone pass them at all.

The man appeared thin, cold and hungry, and wore an old-fashioned costume with a wide-brimmed hat, similar to that of a Quaker. This figure was also seen in 2003 in the early hours by a young father pushing his baby son in a pushchair in an attempt to get him to sleep. The ghost has been witnessed on other occasions near to the old Quaker burial ground, which in itself is a very spooky place. It is located halfway up Port Hill next to the former Reindeer Inn. A local woman once made deliveries in the area before 6 a.m. and, on misty, miserable mornings, she was too scared to go past the burial ground.

fifteen

Hertford Environs

Ladies of the Manor

Leahoe House

Leahoe House stands in the leafy grounds of County Hall. It was built in the mid–1800s for Dr George Elin, but has been owned by Hertfordshire County Council since 1935 as a recreation and leisure centre.

One night after closing time in the late 1980s, Tony Joshua was locking up the bar where he worked voluntarily. Passing through the snooker room at the back of the bar, the hairs on the back of his neck suddenly stood up, his heart raced and for some reason he felt really scared. Walking out into the corridor, Tony happened to look up

Leahoe House. (Hertford Museum collection)

towards the top of the stairs and there stood the figure of a woman in a long black skirt and nun's grey habit. All his feelings of fear drained away and he felt totally at ease. He was transfixed looking at the woman and, when he finally switched the lights off and turned to leave, she was still standing there. Tony has often sensed her presence since that time, although never again has he seen her. He states that this experience changed his sceptical views about ghosts.

Another time, a man was sitting at the bar having a drink when a light from the ceiling flew across the room with no explanation. Also, a young lad was hit in the face by invisible hands and was thrown down the outside steps at the back of the building. A mysterious handprint stayed on his face for four days.

Balls Park Mansion

Looming out of the moonlit darkness is Balls Park Mansion. This spooky seventeenth-century house is the scene of an autumn haunting. Standing in enchant-ing grounds, it has been much altered over time. Balls Park was in the ownership of the University of Hertfordshire until 2003, when it was sold to property developers. From the outside, though, the brooding-looking building is little changed and was a location in the 2005 BBC drama *Bleak House*. It is now residential dwellings.

Balls Park was originally the property of the Willis family, as was Priory Manor. The lavish Jacobean-style wood-panelled vestibule, with its fireplace of Elizabethan origin, is where the haunting takes place.

Late in the evening, many of the university staff reported seeing the resident Grey Lady. In October 2001 a member of staff was leaving at 7 p.m., but, finding the front door to the mansion locked by security, she turned to find another exit and saw a grey figure standing under the balcony in the vestibule. On another misty autumnal night in 2001, a member of the university security staff was walking towards the door of the mansion when he was suddenly flung

Balls Park, showing the southern aspect. (Hertford Museum collection)

backwards several feet by an invisible force. According to local tales, the ghost is that of a lady who threw herself off the balcony from the first floor into the vestibule one October. She has been seen many times during this month in the vestibule and also on the first floor, pacing the corridors.

Hertford Heath

The Many Ghosts of Haileybury College

Maid in the bathroom

Haileybury has many legends of spirits that roam the old school or the buildings connected with it. On one occasion, a bathroom door on the second floor was discovered to have been locked from the inside. It would have been impossible for someone to lock the door and then leave as there was no other exit. In the end, the lock was removed and nothing was found to be wrong with the door.

Perhaps this strange event is connected with the story of the young maid who haunts the third floor, which was once the servants' quarters. She was apparently the victim of a brutal master whose improper attentions caused her to flee and hide in the second-floor bathroom. However, in those days there was no lock, so he was able to open the door; she was trapped, with no way of escaping from him. Could the wraith of this poor girl have locked the bathroom door from the inside, many years after her death?

Nightmarish vision at Colvin House

Between the hours of 2 and 3 a.m. one November morning, two pupils of Colvin House were visited by a nightmarish vision. The first girl claims she was woken by someone shaking her. She opened her eyes and a pale-faced girl with dark hair was standing over her, crying. At first she

Haileybury College Quadrangle, 1900s. (Hertford Museum collection)

thought it was one of her friends, then a feeling of fear and panic overcame her and she fumbled for the light switch. When the light came on, the girl had vanished.

The second girl had woken from a bad dream and she leaned over the bed to retrieve her pillow which had fallen onto the floor. Her eyes fell upon the dark, skinny shadow of a girl looking out of the window. She felt terrified and froze in her bed. The girl then turned away and glanced in a mirror. She seemed to realise the pupil was awake and walked towards her bed before vanishing.

The ghost of Batten-Kipling block

The presence of a young boy who fell from a study window in the Batten-Kipling block is still felt skulking around the narrow passages that connect the houses to the quad.

Spirits of the sanatorium

Alban's House, the sanatorium building, is home to the spirits of students who never recovered from their illnesses. Perhaps the best known is that of a young woman struck down by pulmonary tuberculosis. The woman is thought to have been separated from her family, and emerges only to mourn her own bad luck and to try to escape the building to which she is eternally bound.

Late to chapel

A tradition at Haileybury was that on a Sunday evening all boys had to have made it to chapel before the bell stopped ringing. One Sunday evening in recent years, two of the teachers were walking a dog through the quad along the side of the Master's Lodge next to the chapel. Suddenly the dog froze and began to growl, its hackles rising. It seemed to be snarling at something the two teachers could not see. Then they heard the pounding of dashing feet, as 'someone' sprinted towards the chapel.

Night-time Scene at the Heath

Cromwellian soldiers

A man living in the centre house of a line of old cottages on the top road to Hertford Heath had woken one night and, to his surprise, had found it was broad daylight outside. Looking out of his window, he saw that his garden had been transformed into a wide field, in the middle of which was a dignified-looking man on horseback reading a document to an assembly of what looked like troops in a uniform the resident did not recognise and with old-fashioned weapons. In amongst them stood a man in chains. The resident called a friend to come and witness the extraordinary scene, but by the time she had arrived, all had returned to normal. So what explanation for the peculiar event? History tells us that Cromwell's troops had been encamped in the vicinity, and soldiers were certainly court-martialled and executed for stepping out of line.

In the late 1970s a man was walking his dog in the area of Haileybury College. Suddenly the air was filled with the sound of yelping hounds and out of the undergrowth, striding towards him, was a large number of soldiers, who then stopped and murdered one of their own men. Shaken by what he had witnessed, the onlooker later undertook some local research and discovered that Cromwell's troops had indeed marched along the road where he had encountered the soldiers. The records also reputedly confirmed that a killing had taken place on the spot.

The Goat Inn

One for the boys
Right in the middle of the village green is the Goat inn. Believed to be over 700 years old, the locals claim that a female ghost keeps a friendly eye on things. She seems to favour the male clientele, being a little more wary of females.

Jenningsbury Farm

Tale of the Jenningsbury ghost
Just before Christmas 1785, Benjamin Cherry Esq., an Alderman of Hertford and eminent butcher and dealer in cattle, was talking to his bailiff at his farm in Jenningsbury. After sending his bailiff to turn some persons out of an adjoining field, Cherry threw himself into the moat. The bailiff returned after a short while and, although every method was used to recover Cherry's life, he died, leaving a fortune of £30,000. For many years after, the spirit of this unfortunate man roamed the premises, shaking the well bucket and chains, and otherwise alarming the dwellers of the farmhouse. Sometimes he would appear in the road, frightening the unwary traveller, but according to legend he was never known to be abroad after midnight. Another apparition was rumoured to haunt the same farm. It took the form of the head of a white horse or a cow, and would appear nightly peering over the front entrance gate.

This was not the only ghostly farmyard animal in Hertfordshire. Ghost hunter Elliott O'Donnell recorded the story of a large white sow which was run over and killed in an unidentified lane. The beast's phantasm would approach unsuspecting travellers from behind, grunting and making an 'unearthly noise'.

Ghost Hunter's Notes: Ghostly animals are an often experienced phenomenon, black dogs being the most common (although these are often seen as omens of death rather than the spirits of dead pets). It is not just people and animals that appear as ghosts; there are also many tales of phantom houses or ships.

BAYFORD

Bayfordbury House Estate

Ghost house
Hertfordshire contains many haunted houses, but perhaps more remarkable than any of them is a house which is itself a ghost. In 1984 the Hertford & Ware Local History Society visited the grand eighteenth-century Bayfordbury House. As the society's members departed from the estate, one of them observed a large red-brick Queen Anne house. The house stood three storeys high and had nine small-paned sash windows. An unimpressive door completed the façade. When the woman was offered a lift and got into the car, she turned once more to look at the house. However, it was no longer there. Remarkably, a friend of hers had a similar experience when she saw a Jacobean manor house by the Sacombe Road in Bengeo. Upon retracing her steps, there was no house.

Ghost Hunter's Notes: Ghost houses can be experienced in the same way that replay ghosts can: things from the past that appear to a bystander, only to vanish on closer inspection or double take. There are other explanations that have been given for this kind of paranormal experience, the most common being a 'time slip' or 'retrocognition'.

Bayfordbury House, 1900s. (Hertford Museum collection)

This is where the person experiencing the event is suddenly surrounded by a whole environment from the past, not just one out-of-place person in the modern surroundings. I am also aware of this ghost house; my mother worked at Bayfordbury for many years and heard it often reported that, on dull rainy nights, the house would appear in the field to the right of the exit driveway from Bayfordbury.

BRICKENDON

Blackfield Farm

The notorious Brickendon spirit
On 4 January 1920, a little girl from Blackfield Farm in Brickendon heard rapping noises in her bedroom. Two days later, her brother Norton concluded that a message was being rapped out in Morse code and proceeded to ask questions in return; but it was not the brother the supposed entity wanted to communicate with, it was little Dorothy White herself. Dorothy told the *Hertfordshire Mercury* newspaper:

About a month ago strange rappings were heard on my bedroom wall. We all talked about it because it was so very strange. Then one time he [the spirit] spoke to me down at the fowl house. I thought it was father doing some repairs. I listened again and I heard the words 'don't be frightened, it's only your old chap.'

As she was a lonely girl with very few friends, Dorothy's family believed a spirit had come to keep their daughter company. Dorothy was acquainted with Morse code, having learned it from her brother. She would converse with the spirit for hours on end using a series of raps; it seemed to know everything about the family, although would not reveal its name, save for the initials B.M.

The strange happenings of Blackfield Farm became widely known and a crowd of hundreds would sometimes gather at the farm, hoping for a glimpse of life beyond the veil. The police were called in on more than one occasion to restrain the hordes of inquisitors gathered at the gate. A reporter from the *Hertfordshire Mercury* came at the end of January to 'interview' B.M. He was joined by Councillor Searles and two representatives of London newspapers. The group met with some abusive and abrupt answers to their questions:

Q. Where have you met me before?
A. In Hell.
Q. Where was Mr H born?
A. In bed
Q. When is fine weather coming?
A. When it stops raining.
Q. Can you tell us anything that will help us to live better lives?
A. Shut up!

The party then went downstairs and were treated to an entertaining exhibition of tap dancing from the upper floor. On leaving, a member of the group shouted goodbye up the stairs and the spirit tapped out 'Ta-ta'. Before the evening's activities had taken place, Dorothy's room had been searched thoroughly and any object that was regarded with suspicion was removed. It certainly appeared that this little girl was a spirit medium.

At the beginning of February, Revd Matthew Bayfield, rector of Hertingfordbury and member of the Society for Psychical Research, visited Dorothy. Outside the farm, a large crowd jostled with each other, anxious for the latest in what was becoming an exciting adventure for this small village. At about 10 p.m., an expectant gasp rippled through the crowd as, at length, Revd Bayfield stepped out of the front door to address the sea of hushed faces before him. He took a deep breath before speaking:

It is my conclusion that the raps were not caused by any super-normal means. There was no spirit in the case but on the other hand I am convinced that there was no deliberate fraud on the part of anyone concerned. The patient is often from moment to moment unaware of what he or she is doing and in the present instance I made certain that the girl did produce the raps but it seems probable she was largely unconscious of the fact and it was due to the state of her health.

The crowd began baying and laughing. Reverend Bayfield carried on bravely, 'It is quite possible for a person in a certain state of health to do certain things without knowing, is that clear?' There were shouts of 'Yes' and some jeering. The reverend pleaded with them to leave the family in peace. But the crowd became angry; robbed of their ghost that had been so widely publicised over the previous weeks, they began to demand answers, but Revd Bayfield would not answer their questions.

In a later interview with the *Hertfordshire Mercury*, Bayfield still refused to explain how the rapping had been produced, thus leaving the general public to conclude for themselves whether the Brickendon ghost was real or fake.

A newspaper article in the 1980s blew away the cobwebs concerning the mysterious goings-on at Blackfield Farm by revealing that the Morse code the 'spirit' had been using to communicate was activated by a series of hidden wires running to the house from the front garden. Brother and sister had concocted the ingenious ruse and hoodwinked a great deal of people, including famous writer and spiritualist Arthur Conan Doyle.

Farmer's Boy Public House

Psychic's experiences at the Farmer's Boy

A Hertford girl took a job at the Farmer's Boy pub in Brickendon. Considering herself psychic, it wasn't long before the pub's resident spirits were introducing themselves to her. Every morning when opening up, staff would find the beer pumps turned off and the cellar re-arranged in an old-fashioned style, with kegs lined up on the floor; every day it would need to be reset. Objects would be moved in the kitchen and the ghosts seemed to dislike things on the wall. One of the spirits was a mischievous child that used to sit on the dessert freezer so it couldn't be opened. Staff had to ask politely for the spirit to get off so they could lift the lid.

In one particular bedroom, knocking has been heard on the wall and 'something' even attempted to open the door. When that failed, a figure walked through the wall. One night, the Hertford girl awoke to hear her dog crying at the bottom of the stairs. She went to let it out but the downstairs door was locked and, despite her hammering loudly for it to be opened, no one came, so she and the dog went back up to bed. The room had become freezing cold and the dog was still crying. Shivering, they hid under the bedclothes until about half an hour later, when a friend came upstairs insisting that the door had not been locked at all.

Another night, the girl was sitting in her car outside the pub when she saw the bar lights come on. Knowing everyone was in bed, she watched carefully as someone strode up to the optics and helped themselves to a drink. The figure then came over to the window and, to her horror, she saw it wasn't any of the regular bar staff. She describes the figure as a man in his forties with dark, scruffy, ear-length hair who was staring at her with intense eyes.

The man started talking to her; in her mind she was telling him to leave her alone, but he didn't leave her head until she had driven quite a way from the pub.

In recent times, manager Suzy Berry has reported that a White Lady has been seen under the archway in the corner of the pub's front room.

HERTINGFORDBURY

Old Rectory

Vision at the rectory

On 10 March 1643 a spectral vision was recorded as being seen near the old rectory. It was described as a shining, silver sword hanging in the sky. A contemporary account of this vision describes it as:

> … a shining cloud in the air, in shape resembling a sword, the point reaching to the north. It was very bright as the moon, the rest of the sky being very serene. It began about 11 at night and vanished not till about one, being seen by all the South of England.

Modern-day thinking has likened this to a UFO sighting, but frustratingly little detail remains of this story.

White Horse Hotel

Well haunted!

This fifteenth-century building, now a hotel, is 'well haunted' according to a former manager. Ladies would experience their hair being pulled in the middle of the night in an upstairs staff bedroom. No one liked walking around after dark and a night porter was

The White Horse, Hertingfordbury, 1900s. (Hertford Museum collection)

found one morning looking extremely pale and shaken. When asked what was wrong, he would only say one word: 'Ghost!' From then on he refused to venture upstairs.

The manager would sometimes be walking along the upstairs corridor when something would make him turn. When he looked around, he would always see the same hazy face at the window.

TEWIN

Three Ladies of Tewin

Tewin Water House

Lady Cathcart of Tewin was a notorious character whose strong personality, it seems, has survived the passing of time. Her wraith haunts Tewin Water House between Hertford and Welwyn. A great beauty, the lady married four times and lived to bury each of her husbands. When she married her fourth hus-

Tewin Water House. (Hertford Museum collection)

band, she had inscribed on her wedding ring: 'If I survive, I'll make it five.' Sadly she did not, but attained the advanced age of ninety-eight before being buried in a special vault in Tewin Church which had been made for her first husband, Squire Fleet, in 1789.

Her long life was colourful. The last husband, an Irishman named Colonel Macquire, kidnapped her away to Ireland and held her prisoner for twenty years until his death finally released her, and she came tearing back to her beloved Tewin Water with a strong spirit. Here she lived for another twenty-three years, unmarried.

Her ghost glides ponderously amongst the trees at Tewin Water, reflecting on her adventurous life. A room in the house itself, known as Lady Cathcart's room, has long had the reputation of being haunted by her spirit.

Tewin Church

Doctor Yarborough, rector of Tewin, recorded this story at an unknown date, sometime between 1682 and 1710. His well-respected acquaintance, General Sabine, Governor of Gibraltar, was dangerously ill due to wounds he had suffered at a battle abroad. The General lay awake one night when the curtains at the foot of the bed were suddenly drawn back and, by the light of the candle in his chamber, he saw, with surprise, his wife standing there looking at him. His wife, Lady Hester Sabine, was a lady he greatly loved and was at the time in England. She then faded away, leaving him astounded at this extraordinary vision. He later found out she had died at about the time her apparition had appeared at his bedside. The General himself died in Gibraltar in 1739.

A marble tomb commemorating General Sabine now rests just inside the doorway of Tewin Church; the figure of Lady Sabine, wearing a black cloak with a hood, lingers near the monument. In the early 1980s, two visitors to the church heard the sound of rustling crinoline skirts in the aisle and felt a strong female presence in the bell tower.

Ghost Hunter's Notes: Visions of a loved one appearing at the time of their death is a commonly reported experience. The person will often appear in a dream, or be seen across a space, but will rarely interact with anyone; there seems to be some kind of psychic connection between the two people.

I have no rational explanation for this experience except that it might be related to the idea that we are all linked by a collective subconscious, similar to the idea that was put forward by the psychologist Carl Jung. This collective subconscious would work like a computer network that links us all and allows information to travel back and forth between us. This idea could also explain other phenomena, like the powers that mediums seem to exhibit.

Tewin churchyard

Another local woman, Lady Anne Grimston, is said to have been the despair of her local parson with her unorthodox views on religion. On her deathbed in 1713, she questioned belief in life after death. Folklore has it that she stated, as she lay dying, that if she rose again may seven trees spring from her grave. Today her time-worn tomb can be seen, surrounded by rusted railings and split dramatically by a tree which has grown into seven parts in Tewin churchyard. In the late nineteenth century, Lady Salisbury of Hatfield House took the author Augustus Hare to visit the tomb. Hare recorded in his diary:

It is the most extraordinary sight. Lady Anne Grimston died, and was buried in Tewin churchyard, and over her grave was placed a great altar-tomb, with a huge massive stone slab on the top of it. In a year or two, this slab showed signs of internal combustion, and out of the middle of it – out of the very middle of it – grew a tree, and increased, till, in the time which has elapsed, it has become one of the largest trees in Hertfordshire. Not only that, but the branches of the tree have writhed about the tomb like the feelers of an octopus, have seized it, and lifted it into the air, so that the very base of the tomb is high up now, one with the tree or trees, so are they welded together. Then a railing was put round the tomb, and the tree has seized upon it in the same way, has twisted the strong iron rails like pack-thread, and they

Lady Anne Grimston's tomb of seven trees, Church of St Peter. (Hertford Museum collection)

are to be seen tangled and twirled high in the branches of the tree.

The ghost of Lady Anne herself has been seen often, floating about the churchyard, especially by the bell ringers who are at the church at all times of the night.

Plume of Feathers

Fine array of spectres at the Plume
Built in 1596, the Plume of Feathers pub was once Queen Elizabeth I's hunting lodge. Apparently the building can only ever be used as a pub, not a house, as this is written in the deeds. The cellar was originally the servants' quarters and is now bricked-up but said to be haunted. In 1999, a female member of staff was trapped alone there in the dark after the door refused to open. She explained, 'There is no handle on the outside of the door so it wasn't being held from the bar as a joke. It also just swings back and forth, so is unlikely to have

jammed fast.' Eventually it 'just opened' and she was able to escape. Startled, she tore out of the cellar. Her colleagues swore they had not been playing a joke on her. The ghost of a little girl has been seen by the bar staff at the top of the cellar steps, and beer taps open and close by themselves.

One member of the bar staff said, 'There is an area upstairs I call the sad spot. I don't like to go up there on my own, you can definitely feel it.' Regulars also say that they have felt people brush past them in the men's toilets.

Mark Thomas, the manager at the time, was sitting by the fire one afternoon, enjoying a bit of peace and quiet during closing hours, when he heard a noise behind him. Spinning round, he saw that the candle on Table 8 had lit itself. There was nobody else in the pub and he had extinguished all the candles after the lunchtime shift. Two phantom old men have been seen in the bar, one sitting at Table 8 and the other leaning on the bar and facing the wrong way. He is in fact propping up a long-gone bar which used to face the opposite direction. One of the bar staff feels his name may be 'Dave'; this employee often sees shadows flitting out of the corner of his eye on quiet afternoons when hardly anyone is in.

In the seventeenth century, the body of a woman was discovered behind the fireplace near Table 8. She is said to have been killed by her husband when he returned from two years at sea to find her pregnant. The fireplace is now filled in.

A long table in the restaurant area behind Table 8 is haunted by the figure of a lady with long grey hair wearing a see-through dress; she cackles at the staff. The ladies' toilet also exudes a very creepy atmosphere. Staff believe the ghosts pick on them, making them unnaturally clumsy behind the bar and in the kitchen. The oven also switches itself on every day and, when the chef turns his back, the gas is turned up and time and again the soup is burned because of this mischievous behaviour.

In nearby Tewin Wood, a resident was cleaning her car in the driveway when she became aware that someone was watching her. She looked up and saw a tall blonde lady whom she described as 'pale of face and very beautiful. She appeared dusty and travel-stained and looked frightened. When I asked her if she was lost and could I help, she disappeared. She did not walk away but rather dissolved before my eyes'.

WATERFORD

Long-gone Village Inhabitants

Waterford Church

Waterford is a charming little hamlet just outside Hertford, nestling in peaceful countryside. The church has a fascinating history. Consecrated in July 1872 by Bishop Wilberforce, son of William Wilberforce who abolished the slave trade, its stained-glass design was entrusted to artists William Morris and Edward Coley Burne-Jones: a partnership legendary in the history of art. Dante Gabriel Rossetti also designed a window here, ensuring that this humble little village has the finest collection of Pre-Raphaelite glass in the world.

One day, Mr Ivor Childs was driving past Waterford Church just after midnight with his wife and sister-in-law. He describes the night as being brightly moonlit, almost like daylight.

> As we passed the church a figure in a long white flowing garment suddenly appeared from the churchyard coming towards the road. I slowed down quickly, afraid I might hit this young woman who was bareheaded with beautiful hair and features. But my wife said: 'Don't stop, don't stop it's a ghost.' However, I did pull up to look round and see the figure literally glide across the road into the recreation field opposite and just disappear. We all three saw it!

Mr Childs has driven along that stretch of road many times afterwards but has never seen anything of the like again.

The Waterford road

A young woman living in Hertford often uses the Waterford road when visiting her mother in Stevenage. She has always been what she calls 'psychic' and will regularly see the ghosts of people long gone lining the side of the road, or working in the adjoining fields, all in their contemporary dress. At Waterford, beside the green telephone connection box, she often sees a man in a floppy hat and 1940s khaki-coloured clothes. Further along the route

Waterford. (Hertford Museum collection)

of her journey she has seen three women sitting on the grass verge of Hooks Cross, usually at sundown.

High Road

In the 1970s, a young woman living at No. 46 High Road, Waterford, had two very strange experiences. One night she woke to find a lovely young lady standing over her. She was wearing a long white dress and had long blonde hair. She smiled in a warm and friendly way and stood for some minutes before slipping back into the wall and disappearing. Could this be the same woman in white that was almost run over by Mr Childs? Local legend says that a young woman drowned in the river Beane which ran through the back garden of the house. She is said to appear each year on the anniversary of her death. In the same room, some months later, the young woman saw the ghost of an old lady dressed in possibly Victorian clothes. This time the apparition drifted back out of the door. The witness, now fifty years old, is adamant that neither vision was a lucid dream.

Goldings Mansion

Chimney sweep's demise

In July 1844, a ten-year-old boy went up the flue of the chimney in the Goldings mansion. The boy got stuck and died from suffocation before his soot-covered body could be removed from the chimney. Over 100 years later, chimney sweeps still swore that they could hear his cries. Goldings later became a Dr Barnardo's home, before being bought by Hertfordshire County Council. It has since been converted into luxury apartments.

Goldings, Waterford. (Hertford Museum collection)

Endnote

By paranormal investigator David Lee

THROUGHOUT history, people have been telling tales of the paranormal, whether this concerns spectral Grey Ladies, objects being moved by invisible forces, strange lights, odd noises or even strangely reminiscent phantom scents. These tales provide fascination and fear for people across the globe. Every culture has some form of what we would class as a ghost story, and, no matter how advanced a culture becomes, the idea of unseen or mysterious beings lurking in the dark has never lost its ability to terrify.

From my experience, and potentially to the relief of some readers, 90 per cent of all incidents experienced on ghost hunts or in vigils have natural and mundane explanations. Furthermore, the presence of infrasound, electromagnetic energy, or fumes in the air have all been shown to have psychological effects that can trick a person into believing that someone is watching them or passing them by. So (if you want to) you can feel reassured that any experiences you have had can potentially be explained scientifically. Other readers might be equally happy to hear that, in my experience, there is still that 10 per cent of occurrences that need more investigation: things that happen, or are seen, which defy any logical explanation.

What is a Ghost?

It is my belief that ghosts are able to use energy in the atmosphere to 'power' perceived phenomena. I am sure that everyone has heard a story where, just before a ghost appears in the room, it becomes freezing cold and people can see their breath. This is an example of energy exchange, where the heat in the atmosphere has been taken to power whatever is about to happen. An example which illustrates a ghost's need for energy could be the infamous and oft-reported Grey Lady or White Lady. There have been many reports of this type of phantom from all over the country, and one that I would like to relate is the reported sighting of a transparent grey woman in a cobbler's shop. This report came from the 1950s, but a similar report from the same location in the 1900s described a White Lady, with no report of transparency. My suggestion is that, over time, ghosts lose their vitality, going from something that is indistinguishable from you or I to gradually fading until they become just white, then grey, then transparent, until finally they no longer have any form.

Types of Ghost

What people often refer to as 'ghosts' can be broken down into three distinct categories. The first is the type that I refer to when I use the word ghost; it is often called a 'residual' entity by ghost hunters. These forms can be considered replay ghosts: those that appear at the same time in the same place repeatedly, such as soldiers still walking the battlements of abandoned castles, or monks gliding across fields. These entities appear to have no knowledge of us and do not respond to any attempt to make contact. They appear to only be replaying past events, either continuously or on certain anniversaries. These presences can seem to pass through walls – not because they have supernatural powers but because there were probably no walls in this place in their lifetime. Gliding ghosts are often doing so because their feet are no longer visible as the floor level has risen over the years.

The stone tape theory suggests that the stone of a building, or the land on which it stands, could have magnetic properties and, under certain conditions, events may be recorded onto the stone in the same way that a video camera records images and sounds onto magnetic tape. The theory states that, given the right atmospheric conditions, these images and sounds can play back. Ghosts from events of particularly high emotional energies, such as battles, murders and suicides, are often reported.

The second type of entity is known as an 'active' presence, sometimes also called a spirit. These ghosts appear to be aware. They are often believed to respond to questions, for instance by knocking. This type of entity can include the poltergeist or trickster energies that reportedly move objects around and have sometimes been known to interact with humans by way of a poke or a push, or by creating the sensation of something holding your hand. Not only do these energies display a form of intelligence but they also have some kind of memory. The cause of these phantoms is unknown but it is often thought that they are the departed souls of humans trapped on earth.

Lastly there is a stranger kind of entity, which I describe as an 'elemental'. These are sometimes called earth energies or guardian spirits, and are not of human origin. They are often seen as swirling black masses similar to dense black smoke; black dogs with red eyes; impossibly large humanoid forms often with glowing eyes and/or wings; snakes; wolves; and generally anything considered fearful. These energies are often experienced at ancient sacred sites such as Iron Age burial mounds or other locations of historical significance. They tend to be able to shape-shift and seem to be guarding the area, making people want to leave by taking the form of something frightful and/or filling the atmosphere with a feeling of malevolence. Some believe that these are energies caused by natural energy crossings on the earth such as ley lines, and that ancient folk were aware of the energy so chose these as their sacred sites. But it is my belief that these entities could be created by ritual means. The magicians of ancient times may have been performing rituals during their funerary rites which may, either purposely or unintentionally, have created a guardian spirit. This might sound like hogwash but experiments have been carried out to discover if it is possible to create magical entities. In Tibet there is an ancient magical rite that can create a 'being' of this sort called a tulpa. Reports have claimed that some tulpas have been so believable that villagers think the entity is a new visitor to the village. In 1972, the Toronto Society for Psychical Research (TSPR) began an experiment to create a ghost. They conceived of a man named Philip, a Scottish nobleman with a fictional and purposefully false and impossible history, drew a picture of him and meditated on all of this for a year, after which time they tried to see if anyone could detect the presence of the ghost of Philip. They did this by using séance techniques and mediums from other groups with no prior knowledge of the experiment. The mediums did indeed report making contact with a man named Philip but said that his history made no sense. The entity also started moving objects around the room and answering questions by way of tapping in front of the group, guests and a film crew, supplying answers from this purposely inaccurate history (a Google video search for 'Toronto Society Psychical Research Philip' should produce some video clips from the original footage of the table-tipping experiment, and interviews with people who were present).

Natural Explanations for Ghosts

Electromagnetic fields

It has been observed many times that, during paranormal experiences, electromagnetic field (EMF) readings can spike. The question raised by this observance is: does the ghost cause the EMF spike or does the EMF cause the ghost? In 2000 an experiment was carried out by Persinger, Tiller and Koren,[1] in which a man, who in the past had been subject to what he considered a ghostly experience, was exposed to a complex electromagnetic field across the right hemisphere of his brain. The hypothesis is that high geomagnetic fields that naturally occur in the environment can cause a feeling that could be interpreted as a ghostly encounter. After ten minutes of exposure to this magnetic field, the subject reported experiencing 'rushes of fear', culminating in an experience similar to that of seeing an apparition.

Infrasound

Infrasound is an extremely low frequency of sound that lies in the range below 20Hz. Vic Tandy and Tony Lawrence of Coventry University hypothesised that these low-frequency sound waves could set up vibrations in the human body that '... may under certain conditions create sensory phenomena suggestive of a ghost'. Symptoms of exposure to infrasound can include nausea, depression and the feeling of being watched. Tandy and Lawrence investigated two notorious hauntings in Coventry and discovered that an infrasound wave was present in both of them. These low-frequency sound waves can be caused by many things, including fans, machinery or even just the wind blowing through a small space.

Tiredness

It may come as no surprise that tiredness can be a considerable factor when looking at the causes of alleged ghost sightings. Marvomatis, in his book *Hypnagogia: The Unique State of Consciousness Between Wakefulness and Sleep*,[2] states that hallucinations can occur in the period between consciousness and sleep. These visions are known as hypnagogic hallucinations and are most often experienced just at the onset of sleep, when dreams mix with the usual vision from the eyes and can cause the appearance of otherworldly or out-of-place images. This hypnagogic phase can occur when staying up very late, especially when sleep-deprived over more than one night.

Another thought on sleep hallucinations is based on the brainwave states that can occur when close to sleep. At this level of relaxation, the brain enters the alpha state, which is the same brainwave frequency as that which occurs under deep meditation, and is the state when you are most likely to hallucinate.

Sleep paralysis

Many cultures share very similar stories of night terrors. The usual experience happens like this: you wake up in the middle of the night and are totally unable to move anything apart from your eyes; you may also feel as though there is a heavy weight pushing down on your chest or legs. In the corner of the room you see a dark figure, sometimes reportedly with red eyes. It quickly moves towards you and lies or sits on top of you. These experiences are often extremely disturbing.

Much research has been done on this subject, and what might appear to be an incredibly frightening experience may actually be explainable. When a body goes into REM sleep, the muscles relax and the body attains a form of paralysis; this prevents you from physically acting out dream scenarios and hurting yourself in the process. Sometimes it is possible to wake and become aware before the REM cycle of sleep is complete, hence the body cannot move until it comes out of its paralysis. The entities reported are believed to be the overlaying of dream images with the standard vision, exactly the same as the hypnagogic hallucinations. Circumstances that can increase the likelihood of sleep paralysis are:

Sleeping face up
Recent increase in mental stress
Dramatic and sudden change to lifestyle
Simultaneously being drunk and overtired

An interesting thing to note here is that the word 'nightmare' actually derives from these night-terror experiences; the word 'mare' is a derivative of a Norse or Germanic word for demon, as folklore would have you believe that the night visitor is in fact a demon.

Pattern recognition

The ability to recognise a pattern, especially faces, is one of the first things we gain as a child. This is probably a primal survival instinct. However, this talent for recognising a face can lead to the anthropomorphising of non-living things, like seeing the face of Jesus in the clouds or in slices of toast. The same phenomenon is at play when we look at photographs that appear to have ghostly forms. Simple objects such as smoke, reflections and foliage, among other things, can combine to look like faces to minds that are so astute at this skill of facial detection.

Suggestion/group mind

When conducting a private ghost hunt, I try very hard not to inadvertently give any details to the other investigators about the presumed hauntings, as this can lead to the investigator subconsciously looking for the things I mentioned. It is a more scientific test to see if anyone on the team can match details to the research without prior knowledge. Group mind, as I call it, can come into play during ghost hunts too: one person experiences something and another might have a slightly different take on the circumstances; however, once they have spoken about the event they are likely to assimilate each other's experiences to their own memories and any differences are forgotten. For this reason, and for more accurate results, any shared experiences should be written down separately before individuals discuss the event, as memory has a way of recalling the more exciting elements of an experience and filtering out the differing or less interesting details.

I approach paranormal research with the presumption that none of this is real but with the hope that the truth is more exciting than that. I have examined carefully my beliefs on these matters, so if you were to ask me, 'Do you believe in ghosts?' I would have to answer, 'Put it this way, I am more afraid of the dark now than before I started my research.'

1 M.A. Persinger, S.G. Tiller, and S.A. Koren (2000). Experimental simulation of a haunt experience and elicitation of paroxysmal electroencephalographic activity by transcerebral complex magnetic fields: induction of a synthetic 'ghost'? *Perceptual and Motor Skills*, Vol. 90

2 'The Ghost in the Machine', published in the *Journal of the Society for Psychical Research*, Vol. 62, No. 851, April 1998

Bibliography

Books

Jolliffe, Graham and Jones, Arthur, *Hertfordshire Inns and Public Houses: An Historical Gazetteer* (University of Hertfordshire Press, 2004)

Page, Dr F.M., *History of Hertford* (Hertford Town Council, 1993)

Purkis, Jean, *The Three Acre Triangle: The Story of Hertford's North Crescent* (Hertford Oral History Group, 1999)

Ruffles, Peter; Purkis, Jean; and Jeffery-Poulter, Stephen, *Hertford Through Time* (Amberley Publishing, 2011)

Sangster, Eve, *West Street, Hertford, the First Two Thousand Years* (Hertford Oral History Group, 2003)

Stratton, Ruth and Connell, Nicholas, *Haunted Hertfordshire* (The Book Castle, 2006)

Hertford Museum: Celebrating our Centenary (Rockingham Press, 2003)

Alley and Ditch: St Andrew Street to Castle Street (Hertford Oral History Group, 2006)

Journals

Hertford and Ware Local History Society Journal, May 2011

Newspapers

Hertfordshire Mercury, 1 December 1961 (Hertford Castle); 22 February 2008 (Marshgate Drive); 9 October 2009 (Master's House)

Other

Haileybury website
Discovering Hertford forum
Hertford Museum oral history archive
Hertford Museum photograph archive
Hertford Museum historical gazetteer

If you enjoyed this book, you may also be interested in…

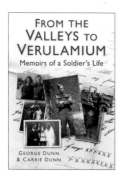

From the Valleys to Verulamium

GEORGE DUNN & CARRIE DUNN

This is the story of George Dunn's life – from Wales to St Albans, to active service a
home again to Hertfordshire. In this poignant book, the author shares vivid memorie
of his life in Hertfordshire and his wartime experiences. From touching recollection:
enjoyable days spent with loved ones to the dark moments of falling bombs, this hor
account is a personal and moving story.

978 0 7524 6508 1

Haunted Bedford

WILLIAM H. KING

From heart-stopping accounts of apparitions and manifestations, to eerie encounters
with phantoms and spirits, this collection of stories reveals Bedford's darker side.
Drawing on historical and contemporary sources, *Haunted Bedford* examines some of
lively characters that are said to haunt the town, including the ghost of famous autho
John Bunyan and Black Tom the highwayman, who was executed here.

978 0 7524 6592 0

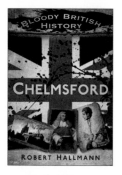

Bloody British History: Chelmsford

ROBERT HALLMANN

This is the bloody, brutal and downright amazing history of Chelmsford. Containing
leprosy, Black Death and rioting peasants; the hideous death of William Caleys; the
reign of terror of the Witchfinder General; the capture of the notorious Coggeshall
gang; and battle against the Zulus, read it if you dare!

978 0 7524 7115 0

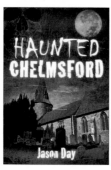

Haunted Chelmsford

JASON DAY

Much of the more sinister history of England took place in Chelmsford, and it woul
seem that many of the participants – and victims – of these events still haunt the to
today. Join author, broadcaster and paranormal investigator Jason Day as he introduce
you to the ghost of an angry nun, a phantom theatre guide and a spectral cyclist.
Encounter the 'Box Monster', the spirits of those women falsely accused of witchcraf
and the mysterious vanishing cloaked figure.

978 0 7524 6221 9

Visit our website and discover thousands of other History Press books.
www.thehistorypress.co.uk